Sabrina wa   cram-
bled onto Santa's lap and told him their most secret
wishes. "Boy, wouldn't it be nice if all I had to do
was ask Santa to give me a job for Christmas?" she
sighed to herself.

That's when she spotted the sign that was posted
on the sleigh that sat in the front of Santa's Workshop. It read:

ELVES WANTED. Inquire Within. Ask for Stan.

This was one job Sabrina knew she was perfect
for. Sabrina knew more about elves than anyone
else in the mall. After all, she'd met a lot of them.
Over the years, she and her aunts had stopped in to
visit Mr. and Mrs. Claus several times. Her first-
hand elf knowledge was going to come in handy.

"Oh, thank you, Santa!" Sabrina shouted with
glee as she raced over toward Santa's Workshop to
apply for the job.

Sabrina, the Teenage Witch™ books

Available from Simon & Schuster

Sabrina The Teenage Witch™

Christmas Crisis

Nancy Krulik

Based upon the characters in Archie Comics

**And based upon the television series
Sabrina, The Teenage Witch
Created for television by Nell Scovell
Developed for television by Jonathan Schmock**

POCKET
BOOKS

LONDON • NEW YORK • SYDNEY

For Connie, Glenn, Mally, and Tess

POCKET
BOOKS

First published in Great Britain 2003 by Pocket Books
An imprint of Simon & Schuster UK Ltd
Africa House, 64-78 Kingsway
London WC2B 6AH

First published in 2003 by Simon Pulse,
an imprint of Simon & Schuster Children's Publishing Division,
New York

POCKET BOOKS and colophon are registered
trademarks of Simon & Schuster
A CIP catalogue record for this book is
available from the British Library

ISBN 0 7434 6258 0

1 3 5 7 9 10 8 6 4 2

Printed and bound in Great Britain by
Bookmarque Ltd, Croydon, Surrey

Chapter 1

"Okay, who wants to choose first?" Sabrina Spellman asked her roommates. She shook her purple-and-blue striped ski cap under their noses. Pieces of folded white paper wiggled around inside the cap.

"Tell me again why we're doing this," Roxie King replied with a decidedly bored tone.

Sabrina wasn't at all intimidated by Roxie's tone. She'd shared a room with her long enough to know that was just how Roxie was. She needed encouragement to try something that wasn't dark and daring. And what Sabrina was proposing was actually something fun and very traditional. Sabrina had been participating in Secret Santa games since she was a little girl. "Because Secret Santa is a Christmas tradition, like mistletoe, and lights, and a big pine tree," Sabrina explained to Roxie.

1

"Oh, you mean like that sad sapling we've got," Roxie moaned, pointing to the scrawny tree Sabrina had placed in the corner of the living room in their off-campus house.

"Oh, it'll look better after I dress it up a little bit," Sabrina assured her. Roxie seemed doubtful.

"No, really," Sabrina said. "I know it's a small tree, but it was all I could afford this year. And you have to have a tree . . . just like you have to have a Secret Santa." She shook the hat in front of her roommates once again.

"Okay, I'll go first," Morgan, one of Sabrina's other roommates, said. She held her perfectly French-manicured fingers over the hat. "Before I pick I just want to remind whoever gets my name that it takes a lot of work for me to look this perfect. My favorite lip gloss color is Rambunctious Red, and I would certainly appreciate a day of beauty at the Zen Zone Spa. Of course for me, every day is a day of beauty because I'm . . . well . . . beautiful, but . . ."

Sabrina rolled her eyes. "Just choose a name, Morgan."

Morgan did as she was told. She pulled out a thin slip of paper, opened it up, and scowled.

"I guess you didn't get the person you were hoping

2

for," Miles, the only male in Sabrina's house, noted.

"Well, I was sort of wishing that . . . ," Morgan began.

"You can't get yourself, Morgan," Roxie snapped, knowing full well that the less-than-generous Morgan would have definitely preferred to buy herself a gift.

"Okay, Miles, you pick now," Sabrina said.

Miles did as he was told. He pulled out a piece of paper, peeked at the name, and then placed it in the top pocket of his shirt.

"Now you, Rox."

Roxie nodded and pulled a name from the hat. She opened it quickly, glanced at the name, and sighed. "Well, I'm glad I've got that new job starting," she remarked. "I'm going to need the extra cash."

Judging from that reaction, Sabrina suspected that Roxie had picked Morgan's name from the hat. But she couldn't tell for sure. And to keep things that way, she made sure to remind her roommates about the rules. "Remember, Secret Santa means keeping your person's name a secret. Don't tell anyone who you picked. That way on Christmas Eve we can all be surprised."

"Is there any price limit on these gifts?" Miles asked.

"Oh, good idea," Sabrina said as she pulled the final name from the hat and kept it for herself.

"How about two hundred dollars?" Morgan asked. "That's the price of a full day of beauty at Zen Zone."

"Two hundred dollars?!" Roxie's voice nervously climbed a scale. "Are you nuts? Who's got that sort of cash?"

"Well, I guess one hundred dollars would be okay. A half day of beauty is better than nothing," Morgan said.

"How about fifty dollars?" Sabrina interrupted. "We should all be able to handle that."

"Well, that's better than two hundred dollars," Roxie agreed. "It's still a little steep, but I can swing it, with my new job and all."

"You don't *have* to spend that much," Sabrina reminded her. "You can come up with a creative gift that costs less. Remember, it's the thought that counts. "

"Yeah, right," Morgan sniffed. "I gotta run. I'm late for a date." She looked in the mirror and started to fix her hair. But she stopped before her fingers ever reached her curly red locks. "Why mess with perfection?" she murmured, blowing her reflection a kiss. "See you guys later."

"I've gotta go, too," Miles said. "I'm late for my astronomy club meeting."

"What are you and the other space cadets discussing tonight, Miles?" Roxie asked him.

"We're calculating the number of minutes until the next sighting of Halley's comet. It's not set to be visible from Earth until 2061, so it could take us all night to figure it out."

"Why don't you just use a calculator?" Sabrina asked him. "You'll have your answer quickly."

"What, and ruin all the fun?" Miles asked. "See you guys later."

"Well, Rox, I guess it's just you and me," Sabrina said. "How'd you like to help me hang some more Christmas lights?"

"Well, much as I'd like to help you use more of our precious energy resources for a trivial purpose, I'm afraid I can't," she told Sabrina. "I have a meeting to go to."

"Oh, what are you saving this time? Whales? Penguins? Amazonian frogs?"

"This meeting's about blueberry smoothies,"

Roxie said. "And strawberry smoothies. Not to mention, the ever popular banana-papaya blend."

Sabrina looked confused.

"It's for my new job," Roxie explained. "I'm working at Sir Smoothie, the all-natural fruit juice bar at the food court in the mall. All the new employees are meeting tonight. They're going to teach us their recipes . . . after they swear us to secrecy."

"What's the big secret to making smoothies?" Sabrina wondered.

"I'll never tell," Roxie replied. "See ya later."

As Roxie left, Sabrina looked around the empty house. She was anxious to start decorating. The question was, where to begin? Finally she settled on getting the tree dressed up. Quickly she grabbed some tinsel and a few small ornaments. She tossed the silver tinsel over a few of the sorry, almost bare, branches. But the tree still looked decrepit. So Sabrina placed a wooden Rudolph the Red-Nosed Reindeer on a low branch.

Plop. The entire tree collapsed on its side under the weight of the tinsel and the one lone ornament.

Sabrina sighed. This was never going to work . . . unless . . .

Sabrina pointed her finger at the tree. Immediately the tree stood back up. Then she pointed her finger slowly toward the roof of the house. The tree began to grow. Thick, sweet-smelling pine needles sprung out from its branches. Within seconds the tree was tall and strong enough to hold all of Sabrina's childhood ornaments.

Sabrina smiled joyously. There were definite benefits to being a witch. She took a few of her ornaments from the box and began to dangle them from the branches of the tree.

Just then the front door swung open. "I forgot my hat. . . ." Roxie began. She gasped. "Where'd that tree come from?"

Sabrina smiled innocently. "It's been here for two days already, Roxie."

"But it was so . . . so . . . so *not that*," Roxie said.

"All it took was a little Christmas magic," Sabrina teased.

Roxie, of course, had no idea that Sabrina was a witch. So the little off-hand comment meant nothing to her. "Whatever," she said. "I've got to hurry." She ran into the room the girls shared and came out a second later with a brown paper bag. "See ya!" she said.

"Deck the halls with boughs of holly," Sabrina sang as she tossed more tinsel on her now-spectacular pine tree.

Sabrina loved holidays—any holidays, from Groundhog Day to Flag Day to National Pickle Appreciation Week. But her two favorite holidays were Halloween and Christmas. As a witch, Halloween was a given. But Sabrina also had a soft spot for Christmas. It was her mother's favorite holiday. Growing up, Sabrina had helped her mother bake cookies, trim the tree, and go caroling—all things mortals did to celebrate Christmas. Sabrina's mother was, after all, a mortal.

Sabrina hadn't been allowed to see her mother very often since she turned sixteen and discovered she was part witch. It was all part of some weird decree sent down by the Witches Council. Celebrating Christmas helped Sabrina feel closer to her mother.

After a little more hot cider and a lot more decorating, Sabrina grew restless. Trimming the tree was more of a team activity than a one-woman job, and she was beginning to feel kind of lonely doing it herself. For a split second, she'd thought about calling Salem to come over for a chat while she worked, but she thought better of it. Salem was a brilliant conversationalist, but he was also presently a cat. And cats seemed to go absolutely crazy around Christmas trees and tinsel. He was liable to pull everything down.

Sabrina walked back over to the stove and ladled some more hot cider from the pot. Then she drifted off into Miles's room. Sabrina had drawn Miles's name from the hat. As his Secret Santa, she wanted to get him something really special—especially since this was Miles's first Secret Santa experience. Unlike Sabrina and her housemates, Miles was Jewish. Although he didn't officially celebrate Christmas, Miles did get into the spirit of gift-giving and joyousness. He'd taught Sabrina and her roommates the Hebrew prayers he said over his Hanukkah menorah, and his mother had sent over some amazing potato pancakes that Miles called *latkes* and jelly donuts he called *soofganiyot*. They were unbelievably yummy!

Miles's room was a definite reflection of his personality. He'd painted the room midnight blue and glued glow-in-the-dark stars all over the ceiling, in perfect constellation formations.

Over by the window, Miles had set up his new

telescope. Miles spent many a night studying the stars and hoping against hope that some visitor from another planet might pass into his sight line. Of course Sabrina knew that the chance of that happening was quite slim—folks from the other planets rarely visited Earth. It wasn't that they were shy; it was more that after you'd seen the Great Red Spot of Jupiter or skied the hills of Mars, Earth seemed incredibly dull.

Sabrina scanned the room, looking for some clue on what to get for her friend. She spotted a catalog sitting on his desk. Something was circled with a red pen.

MIRROR REFLECTIVE TELESCOPE LENS
Gives perfect left and right views of the
night sky. The ultimate in home astronomy
lenses! Now just $49.99.

That was it! Sabrina would get Miles the telescope lens of his dreams. It was within the price range they'd set, and she knew it would make him happy. Quickly she copied down the phone number on the catalog and raced to the phone to order the lens.

"Hello, Close Up Telescope Company," the woman on the other end of the line said. "How may I help you?"

"I'd like to order your mirror reflective telescope lens," Sabrina replied. "You know, the one that's just $49.99."

Sabrina gave the phone operator her credit card number and the expiration date on the card. Then she waited for her card to be approved.

And she waited.

And waited.

Finally the saleswoman from the Close Up Telescope Company came back on the line. "I'm sorry," she said. "Your card has been rejected."

Sabrina was shocked. "What? Why?"

"Apparently you're over your credit limit," the saleswoman told her. "Don't feel bad. That happens to a lot of people this time of year. Have a nice day." With that, the phone line went dead.

"Over my credit limit?" Sabrina muttered as she hung up the phone. "But I haven't even bought any gifts yet. All I did was buy a few decorations. . . ."

Sabrina wandered out into the living room and looked around. Maybe a few wasn't the right word. Sabrina had bought new lights, a dancing Santa, ornaments, and a giant Rudolph the Red-Nosed Reindeer whose nose blinked on and off all night long. Maybe she'd spent more money than she'd thought.

"Now what am I supposed to do about Miles's gift and gifts for my family?" Sabrina moaned to the dancing Santa.

The Santa wiggled back and forth and laughed out loud. "Ho ho ho!" it mocked her.

Sabrina's first thought was to call her Aunt Hilda and ask her for a couple of extra hours of work at the coffeehouse. Sabrina's aunt was the owner of the most popular caffeinated hangout in town, and sometimes Sabrina worked there as a waitress.

But the college was closed for the holiday break, and the coffee house was pretty empty. Hilda really didn't need any extra waitresses on staff. And with so few customers, the tips would be really lousy.

So asking Hilda for work was out. In the first place, her aunt would surely turn her down. And in the second place, Hilda would tell her sister Zelda that Sabrina was over her credit card limit . . . again. Sabrina would then have to sit through a lecture from her Aunt Zelda about budgeting and taking responsibility for her own money. Aunt Zelda had advised Sabrina to put away a little bit each month so that she would have cash for emergencies just like this. But Sabrina hadn't heeded her aunt's warning.

"You look like something I dragged in," a deep voice piped up suddenly from the windowsill.

Sabrina jumped. Then she breathed a sigh of relief. It was just Salem.

"You can't sneak up on people like that, Salem," she scolded him.

"What, too *Scream* for you?" the cat teased. He put on his best scary-movie voice. "I'm calling from inside the house." He laughed.

"Go away," Sabrina instructed, "unless you can solve my problem."

"What is it *this* time?" Salem asked.

"I need some extra cash for Christmas presents. Can you lend me fifty bucks?"

Salem crossed to the tree. "Yeah, that's gonna happen."

Sabrina sighed. She should have known better than to have asked Salem for cash. The cat was such a cheapskate. He never parted with his billfold. "I want to get Miles a telescope lens for a Secret Santa gift, but I've kind of overspent my credit card limit."

"Hello," Salem said. "You're a witch. Just zap him a lens."

Sabrina sat up excitedly. Of course. She could just whip up a lens for Miles. It would be free! It would be . . . a disaster.

"Salem, I can't do that!" she told the cat. "You know what happens when I give magical human gifts. It's always a catastrophe."

"How do you figure?" the cat asked as he lay down beneath the Christmas tree and used his front paw to play with one of Sabrina's new glass ornaments.

"Well, there's no predicting how an Other Realm gift is going to work. I mean, it might be just fine. But Miles could also wind up with a telescope lens that sees through people's clothes or reads their minds."

"Sounds like a lot more fun than watching stars all night," Salem joked. *Smash!* The cat leaped out of the way just before the glass ornament crashed to the floor.

"Salem, go home," Sabrina moaned.

"There is one other thing you could do," Salem suggested as he leaped back up onto the windowsill.

"What's that?" Sabrina asked the cat.

"You could get a job—just for the holidays I mean. You're finished with classes for the semester. You've got plenty of time."

Sabrina leaped up excitedly and hugged the cat. "Thank you! That's a great idea!"

"Just remember who gave it to you when you're cruising the gourmet fish market. . . . Hint, hint."

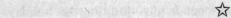

Chapter 2

Sabrina got up extra early the next morning. She wanted to make sure she had a good breakfast before she spent the day job hunting at the mall.

"Whoa! What are you feeding, a small nation?" Roxie asked as she walked into the kitchen and stared at the three eggs, two sausages, and stack of pancakes Sabrina was chowing down on.

"It's the most important meal of the day," Sabrina reminded her roommate.

"Mmm hmm," Roxie murmured as she grabbed a slice of cold pizza from the fridge.

"That's what you're eating?" Sabrina asked her.

"Hey, it's got cheese, bread, and tomato sauce. That's three out of four basic food groups," Roxie replied. She sat down beside Sabrina at the table. "I'm sorry there're no more jobs at Sir Smoothie.

16

It would have been fun working together."

Sabrina shrugged. "That's okay. I'm sure there are lots of other jobs out there. One of them has to be the right one for me."

"That's the spirit," Roxie cheered her. She studied Sabrina's very professional black-and-white checked suit and the way she'd styled her long blonde hair into a tight chignon. "Is that what you're wearing today?"

Sabrina nodded. "Why? Is there something wrong?"

Roxie shook her head. "No, it's very professional. And it would be perfect if you were interviewing at a library or something. But for a job at a mall . . ."

Sabrina looked at Roxie. She was wearing her Sir Smoothie uniform—complete with a hat that looked like a giant smoothie growing out of her head. "I'm not sure you're in any position to give fashion advice," Sabrina said defensively. "Besides, I want the people I interview with to know I mean business. Remember, there are no small jobs, only small—"

"Paychecks," Roxie finished her sentence. "No one ever got rich on a part-time job at the mall."

"I just want to make enough money to buy presents for my Secret Santa and family," Sabrina said.

"I'll be happy when Santa and his elves go back

to the North Pole," Roxie remarked. "I am so tired of hearing about Christmas!"

Sabrina laughed. "Don't worry, Scrooge," she teased. "It'll all be over soon. And then we can look forward to another dateless New Year's Eve!"

Roxie scowled.

Sabrina brushed the crumbs from her suit, tightened the bun in her hair, and headed for the door. "Wish me luck," she said as she headed out to join the workforce.

Sabrina arrived at the mall just as the doors opened, but already the place was mobbed with shoppers. Sabrina had suddenly entered a sea of crying babies, exhausted parents, and overwhelmed shop owners.

There were also plenty of other people at the mall who were searching for holiday jobs. Sabrina could pick them out of the crowd easily. They were the ones who weren't carrying packages. Instead they had their pens out and at the ready for filling out those all-important job application forms.

Sabrina glanced over toward the Beans and Cobalt Bookstore. There was a HELP WANTED sign right in the window. Sabrina smiled. A job in a bookstore! What could be more perfect? Sabrina

loved to read, and she never tired of recommend-
ing books to her friends—whether they wanted the
recommendations or not. Now she could get paid
for doing exactly that.

Sarbina put her hand in front of her mouth and
breathed. Yuck! Time for a mint. Quickly she
popped a peppermint candy in her mouth, smoothed
out her skirt, and walked into the bookstore.

Unfortunately, before she could even get in the
door, she saw the manager of the store take the HELP
WANTED sign from the window. She watched as the
manager shook the hand of a tall, thin college-age
guy who was obviously his new employee.

Darn it! If she'd just gotten there a few minutes
sooner, Sabrina was sure that the job would have
been hers! But Sabrina wasn't one to dwell on the
past. She was determined to get a job. Any job.
She'd just have to keep looking.

A few doors down, Sabrina spotted another sign
in a shop window. Without even looking to see what
sort of shop it was, she burst in the door, ready to
wow the manager. She walked up to the counter,
smiled brightly, and said, "I'd like to talk to the
manager about the job."

The short, chubby woman behind the counter

looked especially happy to see Sabrina. "I'm the manager," she replied, "and you're hired."

"What?" Sabrina asked, surprised. "Don't you want to hear about my past employment, or talk to my references, or even just know my name?"

"Look, I've gone through six employees in the past two weeks. And this is our busiest season. I don't have time for small talk. If you want the job, grab your uniform and that tray of cheese, and start handing out the samples to the customers."

It was only then that Sabrina noticed the odd stench in the store. The smell was sour and aged—like bad cheese. She glanced at the name written on the plastic bags that sat behind the corner. Svenson's Cheese Emporium.

Okay, so pushing cheese to customers wasn't quite as romantic as working in a bookstore, but as Roxie would say, the cash was just as green.

"I'll take the job," Sabrina assured the woman. "And I don't know why your other salespeople didn't work out, but I assure you that I will. . . ."

"Yeah, yeah, whatever," the woman said. "Just go in the back. Joe's there doing inventory. He'll help you find your uniform. Then put it on and help out with the customers."

Sabrina did as she was told. She hurried to the back of the store. There she was greeted by a lanky strawberry-blond haired guy with a beet-red nose. He was wearing blue jeans, a denim shirt, and a plaid apron. He definitely had that dairy farm look about him.

"Huddo," he greeted her, his voice sounding raspy and stuffy, like he had a cold. "I'm Joe."

"Sabrina. Pleased to meet you." She held her hand out to him.

But before Joe could shake, he pulled out a tissue. "Kerchoo!" he sneezed.

"Bless you," Sabrina replied. "Are you okay?"

"It's just a little cold," Joe said. "I've been like this for at least a month now. Can't smell a thing."

Sabrina sniffed at the air. The smell of cheese was overwhelming. "Lucky you," she assured him.

"Huh?"

"Never mind," Sabrina replied. "I'm the new employee, Sabrina Spellman. The woman behind the counter said you could help me find my uniform."

"That's Ida," Joe said between sniffles. "She owns this place."

"How long have you been working here?" Sabrina asked Joe.

"About a month," Joe answered.

"Oh, that's interesting, because Ida told me that she'd been through six employees in two weeks."

"Kerchoo! I know," Joe replied as he sorted through a few boxes looking for Sabrina's uniform. "I can't understand why they left. Ida's really nice. Aah. Here's your uniform."

Sabrina expected Joe to pull a pair of jeans and an apron from the box, just like he was wearing. But Sabrina's uniform was very different.

Her uniform was a black-and-white cow costume—complete with big pink plastic udders on the belly.

"I have to wear that?" Sabrina gasped.

"You're the Svenson Cow," Joe told her. "The mascot of the store. Didn't Ida tell you that?"

"She never mentioned it," Sabrina answered.

"It's an honor," Joe assured her. "They don't let just anybody wear the cow suit." He pointed to a small employee washroom. "You can change in there."

Sabrina really didn't want to wear a cow costume. It was demeaning; it was embarrassing; it was . . . *a job*. And that was what Sabrina needed at the moment. *Beggars can't be choosers,* she thought to herself as she took the costume in her arms and went into the washroom to change.

"Okay, I'm ready," Sabrina said as she reentered the stockroom. "How do I look?"

"Kind of creepy," Joe told her.

Sabrina scowled. "You wouldn't exactly look like a fashion model, either, if you were wearing this suit."

"That's not what I meant," Joe said. "It's just that you have a cow body and a human head. It's a weird combination." He handed her a giant cow head. "You have to look exactly like Svenson."

Sabrina sighed. This was going from bad to worse. Still, unless she wanted to be begging for money from her aunts, or worse yet, Salem, she'd better put on the head. Slowly she lifted the big cow head in her arms and placed it over her head.

It was hot inside the cow costume. And the tiny eye holes were not nearly big enough for Sabrina to see through. Still, she was able to somehow make her way out of the stockroom and into the main store.

"Just pick up any tray of cheese and start handing out samples," Joe told her. "I'd do it myself, but people get grossed out when I sneeze on the cheese." He laughed. "I just love that rhyme."

"Wow! Mommy, look at the cow," a little boy yelled when he spotted Sabrina.

"Why don't you go play with the cow while Mommy buys a nice cheese log for the party," his exasperated mother replied. She seemed incredibly pleased to have someone else entertain her son for a few moments.

The little boy raced over to Sabrina, his arms open wide. For a moment, she thought he was going to give her a hug. *This is too sweet,* she thought to herself.

But hugging wasn't at all what the boy had in mind. Mauling was more like it. First he bashed into Sabrina's pink plastic stomach. Then he yanked on her udders. "Look, Mommy! I'm milking the cow!" he called out.

"That's nice, dear," his mother murmured, paying absolutely no attention to her son at all.

The boy soon got tired of milking the cow. Now he decided to yank on its tail. He pulled hard, nearly throwing Sabrina onto the floor. It was hard enough to keep her balance with the huge cow head on her shoulders. She didn't need this kid tormenting her, too.

"Hey, that's not nice!" Sabrina hissed from beneath the cow head.

The little boy stared at the cow for a moment, his eyes open wide. Then suddenly he let out a huge wail. "AAAHHHHH! Mommy, the cow yelled at me!"

His mother sighed and walked over toward Sabrina. "Did you yell at my son?" she demanded.

Before Sabrina could reply, Ida came hurrying over. "Is there a problem?" she asked.

"This cow just yelled at my kid," the woman snapped.

"But he—" Sabrina began.

"I'm sure the cow didn't yell," Ida assured her. "Svenson is a loving cow. *And she doesn't speak a word.*" She turned to Sabrina. "Give this nice boy a cheese stick, Svenson," Ida told Sabrina, pointing to a display of a log cabin built of mozzarella sticks.

Sabrina took the boy by the hand and brought him over to the cabin. She handed him a stick of cheese.

"Excuse me, can you help me?" A tired-looking man in a blue overcoat tapped Sabrina on the shoulder.

She turned around quickly. The cow head tipped precariously on her neck. Sabrina straightened her head and nodded slowly.

"Can you cut me a nice hunk of Limburger cheese?" the man asked.

Sabrina went behind one of the cheese counters. She walked slowly, trying not to concentrate on just how hot it was inside the cow costume. Then she scanned the counter, looking for the Limburger.

As she pulled the cheese from the counter, the pungent scent of Limburger wafted under her nose. The heat from the cow costume became overwhelming. The combination of stinky cheese and overwhelming warmth took her over. The room began to spin in front of her eyes, and . . . *boom!* She fell to the floor with a thud.

When Sabrina opened her eyes again, the little boy who'd pulled her tail was screaming in the ear of the cow costume. "Mommy! The cow's dead!" he cried.

Sabrina struggled to sit up. She lifted the hot cow's head from her shoulders. The little boy couldn't believe his eyes. Seeing the cow lose its head was too much for him. He began to scream. Everyone in the store turned to stare.

"Now look what you've done! You've traumatized my child. What were you thinking?" his mother demanded.

"But I fainted," Sabrina said weakly. "I couldn't breathe and it was so hot in there and—"

"You couldn't breathe? Is that your excuse for upsetting a little boy? How inconsiderate," the mother scolded Sabrina. She grabbed her son and took him from the store. "We're taking our business elsewhere."

"Please, ma'am," Ida trailed after her. "I'm sorry. It's just that it's so hard to get good help these days."

That was more than Sabrina could take. There was no amount of money worth this. She stood up, handed Ida the cow's head and said, "I don't think this going to work out."

As Sabrina walked into the stockroom to get back into her clothes, she could hear Ida mutter, "That one didn't even last an hour. I wonder why all my cows keep leaving?"

A few minutes later Sabrina found herself back pounding the pavement searching for a job. The mall was even more crowded now. But that didn't seem to be affecting Sabrina one bit. Everywhere she walked, people moved away, clearing a path for her.

At first Sabrina didn't seem to notice this odd behavior. But then she heard two teenagers whispering behind her back.

"Man, she stinks!" one teen said.

"Yeah, she smells like Limburger cheese!" the other replied.

Sabrina gasped. *Oh no!* The cheese store had left its awful mark on her. She couldn't go on a job interview smelling like the stinky cheese girl. But she didn't have time to rush home and shower and change. For a moment she considered using magic to clean herself up, but there was no empty place anywhere in the mall where she could hide and point.

At that very moment Sabrina passed by Scents for Cents, a discount perfume store. Quickly she dashed into the store and headed over to the counter.

"May I help you?" the woman behind the counter asked, taking care to keep her distance from Sabrina.

"I'd like to try a perfume," Sabrina told her.

"Any scent in particular?" the woman asked.

Sabrina shook her head. "No. I just want a really strong one."

The saleswoman handed Sabrina a sample bottle of perfume. "Try this," she said, wrinkling her nose. "Try lots of it."

Sabrina did exactly that. She sprayed herself from head to foot with the sweet-smelling perfume. Then, when she was certain that she'd completely masked the scent of cheese, she handed the bottle back to the saleswoman. "Thanks," she said.

The woman nodded and took the sample back behind the counter. "Don't mention it," she told Sabrina.

Now that she was certain that she looked and smelled like a potential employee, Sabrina took on a renewed sense of purpose. She'd find the right job. She was sure of it. The trick was finding a job that was just her style.

Sabrina walked past the food court. For a moment she thought about seeing if any of the small fast-food restaurants were looking for help. But her experience with the cheese had pretty much put her off that idea.

Instead, she wandered into a high-priced dress shop on the second floor of the mall. The sign in the window said EXPERIENCED SALESWOMAN NEEDED. Sabrina didn't have any experience selling dresses, but she did have some sales experience. After all, she'd just spent forty-five minutes selling cheese.

"I'd like to apply for the saleswoman job," Sabrina told a tall, elegant, fortyish woman behind the counter.

The woman smiled kindly at Sabrina. "I'm awfully sorry dear, but that position has just been filled."

Sabrina looked devastated. "But the sign . . ."

"I know, I was just about to take it out of the window." The woman noted Sabrina's sad look and then studied her suit and her hairdo. "But actually, I do have a job open that you would be absolutely perfect for—although it's just one day's worth of work."

Sabrina thought about that. One day's work was better than nothing. And she could always find another job after that. "I'll take it!" she said quickly.

The woman laughed. "You don't even know what the job is," she said.

Sabrina blushed. "Oh, right. What do I need to do?"

"Well, you see, we're giving a special seminar on fashion do's and don'ts. And your suit, hairstyle, and unique taste in perfume would be a perfect example."

Sabrina smiled brightly. This woman, who obviously knew a lot about fashion, appreciated her look. She couldn't wait to rush home and tell Roxie. Her roommate had been totally wrong. Sabrina's outfit was the perfect example of a professional look.

"That sounds fantastic," Sabrina said. "I just knew you'd like this suit. You know, I put this whole outfit together myself. And I copied the hairstyle from a magazine. I guess I just have a certain flair for fashion."

The saleswoman frowned slightly and tried to look as kindly as possible into Sabrina's eyes. "Well, actually, dear, I was thinking you could be our fashion *don't* model. That look is completely wrong for you. You need softer hair, and that suit is . . . well . . . it's not the look we go for in this store."

Sabrina could feel the tears building up in her eyes. First she had to dress like a cow, and now this woman was telling her that she was a fashion disaster! Who knew searching for a job could be so humiliating?

Without even saying a word, Sabrina turned and ran from the dress shop.

"Was it something I said?" the woman in the dress shop called after Sabrina.

Sabrina kept walking faster and faster through the mall. Her cheeks were burning with embarrassment, her nose was tingling from the smell of the strong perfume, and her head hurt from the tightness of the bun in her hair.

This had been quite possibly the worst day of her entire life . . . and it wasn't even noon yet!

Sabrina sat down on a bench, rested her weary feet, took a deep breath, and looked out at the busy mall. Suddenly, despite the pressures of the day, a small smile began to form on her face. She saw at least a hundred children smiling and waiting impatiently for something exciting to happen.

They were about to meet Santa.

An entire Santa's Workshop had been set up in the center of the mall. It was sort of funny—white cotton had been glued to white cardboard to make fake snowdrifts, mechanical reindeer moved back and forth alongside a big throne that had been spray-painted gold, and a tired, beleaguered mall Santa sat on the throne, staring aimlessly into space as yet another child crawled onto his lap and told him what he wanted for Christmas. To an adult eye, it was obviously a fake backdrop for a photograph. But to the children, it was magical. It was obvious to Sabrina that the children who had been brought to the Santa's Workshop display would never forget the day they'd met Santa Claus.

Sabrina watched enviously as happy children scrambled onto Santa's lap and told him their most secret wishes. "Boy, wouldn't it be nice if all I had to do was ask Santa to give me a job for Christmas?" she sighed to herself.

That's when she spotted the sign that was posted on the sleigh that sat in the front of Santa's Workshop. It read:

ELVES WANTED.
Inquire Within. Ask for Stan.

This was one job Sabrina knew she was perfect for. Sabrina knew more about elves than anyone else in the mall. After all, she'd met a lot of them. Over the years, she and her aunts had stopped in to visit Mr. and Mrs. Claus several times. Just last February, Sabrina and her aunts had gone skiing at the North Pole during her winter break. There were plenty of elves at the ski resort. February was their off-season, and they'd had plenty of time to slalom down the slopes. At the time, Sabrina had wished that she could have been in Florida with her friends getting a tan, but now she was glad she'd opted for the family vacation. Her first-hand elf knowledge was going to come in handy.

"Oh, thank you, Santa!" Sabrina shouted with glee as she raced over toward Santa's Workshop to apply for the job.

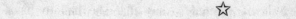

Chapter 3

☆

"So, how did the job hunting go?" Roxie asked when Sabrina returned to the house late that afternoon.

"Great!" Sabrina exclaimed. "I got a great job, working as an elf at Santa's Workshop. I start tomorrow."

"So you're going to be helping a fake symbol of the commercialization of Christmas and fool innocent children into believing that the holidays are all about their wish lists," Roxie mused.

Sabrina frowned. The job didn't sound so wonderful when you put it that way. "Actually I just help Santa get the kids to smile while the photographer shoots their pictures."

"What kind of qualifications did you need for that?" Roxie asked her.

Sabrina wanted to say that she had to have a cheerful disposition and a love of children, but that hadn't been the truth. "I fit the suit," she admitted to Roxie.

Roxie laughed. "What is it with these costumes? When I first started looking for jobs, I applied for one in Svenson's Cheese Emporium. But they wanted me to dress up like a cow. What kind of jerk would agree to do that?"

Sabrina blushed. "I can't imagine," she said. "Anyway *this* uniform is cute." She reached into her bag and pulled out a red leotard, white skirt, and red tights. Then she placed a red and white felt hat on her head. "I feel so Christmasy!" she said excitedly.

"You do look like you've got the Christmas spirit," Roxie agreed. "Or you could be a giant tomato."

Sabrina frowned. "You're just jealous because I don't have to wear a giant smoothie on my head."

Roxie shrugged. "I have to admit working at Sir Smoothie isn't what I thought it would be. They're not what they pretend to be."

"What do you mean?"

"Never mind," Roxie replied. "By the way, your Aunt Hilda called. Your cousin Amanda sent you a gift and Hilda wants it out of her house immediately."

"Did she say why?" Sabrina asked.

"I think she said something about it growling too loud. What could that possibly mean?"

"With Amanda, it could mean anything." Sabrina sighed. Her cousin Amanda was known for her practical, and often dangerous, pranks. In the past she'd shrunk Sabrina to the size of a moth and held her prisoner in a glass jar. She'd also once turned Sabrina's high school boyfriend Harvey into a dog—and those were the mildest of her impractical jokes. "I'd better go over and check it out," Sabrina said as she hustled out the door.

"Aunt Hilda, Aunt Zelda?" Sabrina called out as she entered her aunts' house. "Anybody home?"

There was no answer. Obviously Zelda and Hilda were busy elsewhere—*hopefully buying me something wonderful for Christmas,* Sabrina thought gleefully.

But her glee turned to groans as she discovered Amanda's gift in the middle of her aunts' living room. It wasn't hard to figure out which box it was—there was only one package that was rocking back and forth, growling like a dinosaur, and giving off the odor of a zoo.

Sabrina held her breath and carried the box upstairs. She took a permanent marker, scribbled "Return to Sender" on the package, and threw it into her aunts' linen closet. In most cases that would have accomplished little more than making the closet full of smelly sheets. But in the case of the Spellman sisters' house, the linen closet actually served as a portal to the Other Realm. Once the box passed through the portal, the Other Realm Post Office would know where to deposit Amanda's gift.

As Sabrina turned and got ready to head back downstairs, she noticed a light flashing behind the door of her old bedroom.

That could mean only one thing. Salem was up to something. And knowing Salem, that something was no good.

"Salem, what are you doing?" Sabrina demanded as she threw open the bedroom door. But before the cat could answer, Sabrina burst out laughing. The cat was wearing a bright red, kitty-sized Speedo bikini bathing suit, standing on his hind legs, and flexing the little kitty muscles in his front legs.

"Is something funny?" Salem asked, dropping to all fours.

Sabrina laughed harder.

"I'll have you know that I've always been considered quite the muscle man," Salem assured her.

"You're not any kind of man," Sabrina reminded him. "You're a cat."

"That's just temporary," Salem insisted

"You consider one hundred years temporary?" Sabrina teased. "So, what's going on here?"

Salem pointed to a camera he'd set up on a tripod across the room. "I've got a camera on a timer. And it's wasting film taking pictures of your backside. Move." The light flashed as the camera clicked again.

The cat got back up on his hind legs and flexed his muscles as though he were a participant in an all-feline Mr. Universe contest.

Sabrina walked over to the desk and picked up a slip of paper. "Macho Male Favorite Familiars Calendar Contest," she read aloud. "Salem, don't tell me you're trying to be a pinup for this thing!"

"Why not?" Salem asked her. "Just think of the babes who would want to get familiar with this familiar when they see this sleek physique."

Sabrina burst out laughing as he sucked in his well-fed tummy to create a "sleek physique." Well, Salem *was* now a familiar, or an animal who served and protected witches. Of course, it had been his own fault. Salem Saberhagen had been a witch. But he had his powers revoked and had been sentenced to one hundred years in the form of a cat after the Witches Council caught him plotting to take over the world. Part of his sentence was to be the pet in the Spellman sisters' household—although at times it was hard to tell just who was being punished by that part of the Council's decree.

"I'm going for Mr. July," Salem told her as he switched poses.

"Which explains the swimsuit," Sabrina replied.

"Oh, you're quick," Salem snapped sarcastically. He held his head up high and turned it from side to side. "Which do you think is my best side?"

"Try turning your back to the camera," Sabrina joked.

Salem hissed.

Sabrina glanced at the entry form. Salem had typed all of his pertinent information. That was no easy task when you considered that his paws didn't have moveable fingers. When Sabrina's eyes reached the hobbies portion of the form, she started laughing again. "Snowboarding? BMX biking? Rock climbing? Come on, Salem, you've never done any of these things."

"I have too," Salem said.

"Slipping on the ice in the driveway does not qualify as snowboarding," Sabrina differed. "And riding in the basket of Aunt Zelda's bicycle does not qualify as BMX biking."

"Picky, picky," Salem replied sarcastically. Then he changed his tone. "You won't tell the judges that I exaggerated—slightly, I might add—will you, Sabrina?"

Sabrina shook her head. "It's not my business what you tell them."

"Exactly," Salem said.

Sabrina looked at the paper again. But the information she was seeking didn't seem to be written anywhere on the form. "So just how much money do you get if you're chosen for the calendar?" Sabrina asked the cat.

"None," Salem said. "All the profits go to a home for aged witches."

Sabrina was surprised to hear that such a place even existed. Since witches could live for centuries without seeming to age much, it was hard to imagine any witch being aged enough to move to a nursing home. "How old do you have to be to live *there*?" she asked.

"Well, let's just say that the current residents were the ones who spread the news about that little invention we now call fire," the cat replied.

"Okay, so you're not in this for the cash," Sabrina thought aloud. "But there's definitely something in it for you. There always is."

"Sabrina, I'm shocked that you would suspect such a thing," Salem said with mock disbelief.

Sabrina spotted a second calendar under the first. It was all *female* familiars. "Let me guess. There's a party or something for all of the pinups, so you're hoping to get a date out of this?"

"Not *a* date, *twelve* dates," Salem corrected her. "Not to mention twenty-five free copies of the calendar."

"When does the calendar come out?"

"It takes a whole year to put it together. That means I'll get my copies just in time for next Christmas. My Christmas gift gathering will be finished early next year . . . and for free."

"You're planning on giving out calendars with a

picture of yourself in them for Christmas?" Sabrina sighed.

"Yes, and you'll only get one if you're good," Salem said.

"What are you giving out *this* year?" Sabrina asked.

"Here's a hint: Just remember it's the thought that counts."

Sabrina shook her head. That didn't sound too promising. Last year Salem had poured clear glaze over some furballs and tried to pass them off as sculptures. The year before that he'd unraveled one of Sabrina's sweaters and tried to give it back to her as a ball of knitting yarn. It was hard to imagine what the Scrooge-like cat could do to top that. "I'll be waiting," she murmured.

"So did you get a job?" Salem asked.

Sabrina nodded excitedly. "At the Santa's Workshop in the mall. I'm an elf."

Salem laughed. "I always thought your ears looked a little pointy."

"At least *my* ears aren't covered in fur," Sabrina shot back.

Usually Salem would have had a snappy comeback for Sabrina. But today he was in a different frame of mind. "It's these furry ears that are going to melt the hearts of the female judges of the Macho Male Favorite Familiars calendar. Not to mention my heart-stopping yellow eyes and roguish charm."

Sabrina rolled her eyes. What Salem might have been lacking in muscles and honesty, he definitely made up for in attitude, or as he called it, cattitude.

"Sabrina, do you mind leaving now?" the cat asked her. "I'm trying to work with the camera, and you're ruining the vibe."

At first Sabrina was fuming. This was her old room. What right did Salem have to kick her out? But then Sabrina decided not to let the cat get to her. Sabrina was in happy holiday mode. Nothing and no one in the world could ruin that!

Chapter 4

"**O**kay, all you have to do is get the kids to smile when they get on Barney's lap," Stan, the photographer at the mall's Santa's Workshop display told Sabrina when she arrived for her first day of work.

"Barney?" Sabrina asked, confused.

"Yeah, that's the name of the guy who's playing Santa this year," Stan explained.

"Okay."

"I don't care how you do it," Stan continued. "Just get those kids to grin. No one wants to buy a picture of their kid having a temper tantrum on Santa's lap. And keep the line moving. We have a lot of customers here, and we don't want them getting frustrated and leaving."

Sabrina looked at the long line of kids who had already gathered to sit on Santa's lap. They all

seemed excited and happy to be there. "No problem,
Stan."

"Oh, and by the way, if you have any friends who
could use a part-time job, I need someone to take
orders for the photos," Stan said.

"Well, everyone I know has a job right now, but
I'll pass on the word," Sabrina assured him.

Stan walked over toward his camera. "Ready to
face the customers?" he asked.

Sabrina nodded eagerly.

"Okay then, let's bring in the kids," Stan said.

Sabrina walked over to the little girl at the front of
the line. "Are you ready to meet Santa?" she asked
her.

The girl looked at Sabrina wide eyed. She nodded.

"What's your name?" Sabrina asked her.

"Emily," the girl replied shyly.

Sabrina took Emily by the hand and brought her
up to where Barney was sitting on his throne.

"Okay, hop up on Santa's lap," Sabrina said.

Emily did as she was told.

"Have you been a good little girl?" Barney the
Santa Claus asked her.

"Sort of," Emily admitted. "I mean, I was nice to

everyone, except my cat. I kinda used his tail as a jump rope for my dolls. He didn't like that very much."

Sabrina thought about how Salem might react if she'd tried that. She wasn't surprised Emily's cat hadn't enjoyed having his tail used as gym equipment.

"Well, do you promise not to use your cat's tail as a toy from now on?" Santa asked her.

Emily nodded.

"So what do you want for Christmas?" he asked.

"A different cat," Emily said. "I didn't promise not to play with a different cat's tail."

"How about a real jump rope?" he asked her.

"Well, it's not as good as a cat. . . ." Emily began.

"Okay, everybody smile," Sabrina said, remembering what Stan had said about keeping the line moving.

Emily smiled broadly. Stan snapped the shot.

"Okay, next," he told Sabrina.

Sabrina went back to the line and tried to take the hand of the next child in line. He looked about eight years old, and he was dressed immaculately for his holiday photo in a little navy blue suit, white shirt, and red tie.

47

"What's your name?" Sabrina asked him.

"Joseph Minton the Third."

"Oh, does your family ever call you Tres?" she asked. "You know, for being the third?"

"They wouldn't dare," replied Joseph Minton III.

"You look very handsome," Sabrina complimented him. "Did your mother pick out that suit?"

"No," Joseph responded in a tone that implied he wasn't impressed with Sabrina's small talk. "I picked this out. It's a power suit."

"A power suit?"

"Yeah, you know, like the guys on Wall Street wear. If you're going to go into negotiations, you have to dress like you're in the power position."

Sabrina was surprised. "You're going into negotiations with Santa?"

"I don't want to go into this with the staff," Joseph told her in a very dismissive tone. "I'd rather discuss my business with the big guy directly." He hopped right onto Santa's lap and unfurled a long list. "Okay, here's the deal. I would like a horse for Christmas. Not just any horse, mind you, a thoroughbred."

"You like to ride horses?" Santa asked.

"No, I want to breed them. And possibly race

them. That's where the real money is. Now I realize that a thoroughbred is a tough gift for you to get under my tree. But I'll make it worth your while. How about I give you my new baby sister in exchange?"

Santa didn't know what to say. He just stared at the mini mogul on his lap.

"Okay, everybody smile," Sabrina cried out, trying to get Joseph off Santa's lap before he made the jolly old guy sign a contract.

The rest of the morning was relatively uneventful. There were a few leaky babies, and one little girl who only spoke Polish, but for the most part, Sabrina got everyone on and off Santa's lap with big smiles and limited stress. But by noon, her feet were killing her, her mouth was frozen in a permanent smile, and she had pieces of a sticky lollipop embedded in her hair. So it was a relief when Stan told her that she could take a lunch break.

Sabrina headed straight for the food court and bought herself a big hamburger, fries, and a soda. She took a seat at a small table and immediately began to chow down. But she hadn't take three bites of her burger when suddenly she heard shouting coming from one of the restaurants.

"How can you say you're all natural?" a familiar voice shouted. "You use artificial sweeteners. Not to mention the fact that you serve drinks in Styrofoam cups! Styrofoam isn't biodegradable. It will exist forever, filling garbage dumps all over the world. Do you know what that does to the environment? You really should be more careful about these things."

Sabrina sighed. She'd know that voice anywhere. Obviously Roxie wasn't doing as well with her new job as Sabrina was doing with hers.

"What I should be more careful about is who I hire," the manager of Sir Smoothie bellowed. "You're fired. Turn in your Smoothie cap."

"With pleasure," Roxie snapped back.

Sabrina bit into her hamburger. She wanted to finish her lunch and get out of the food court before Roxie spotted her. It wasn't that Sabrina didn't feel bad for Roxie or that she thought Roxie was completely wrong in insisting that the management of Sir Smoothie be more ecological and health minded—especially since they billed themselves as all-natural. It was just that Roxie could be very unpredictable when she was this angry. Sabrina wanted to give her a while to calm down before she spoke to her.

No such luck. Roxie spotted Sabrina across the food court. As soon as she turned in her hat and her apron, she raced over and plopped down in the seat across from Sabrina.

"You'll never believe what just happened," Roxie moaned.

"You had a fight with your manager and you got fired," Sabrina replied.

"Oh," Roxie said, "you heard?"

"I think the only person who didn't hear you is some fisherman in the Atlantic Ocean near Portugal," Sabrina said.

"Well, I was mad," Roxie defended herself. "And I was right."

"Yes, you were," Sabrina agreed. It was always best to agree with Roxie when she got like this.

"But I'm also out of a job," Roxie moaned.

"Yes, you are," Sabrina agreed again.

Roxie grabbed a few of Sabrina's fries and leaned back in her chair. "So how's your job going?" she asked.

"Um, it's okay."

"Not great?"

Sabrina didn't know how to answer. She liked her job. But Roxie certainly didn't want to hear that right now. "It's a Christmas job," Sabrina said finally.

Roxie nodded. "They wouldn't happen to need any more elves over there, would they?"

Sabrina gulped. Stan had mentioned that he wanted someone to take photo orders. But the idea of someone like Roxie working in Santa's Workshop wasn't exactly what Sabrina thought he'd had in mind.

"No, they don't need any *elves*," Sabrina replied. There, that hadn't been a total lie. After all, it wasn't elves that Stan needed.

"How about a bouncer then?" Roxie asked. "Someone to keep the pushy parents in line?"

Sabrina laughed. Roxie was right. Some of the parents were pushy. Luckily most of their kids were sweet. Sabrina shook her head. "I don't think we need bouncers."

"Have you seen any other jobs around the mall then?" Roxie asked her. "I mean, that don't require you to dress up as farm animals."

Sabrina sighed. She was a lousy liar and a good friend. She didn't want to keep secrets from Roxie. "Well, there is *one* job at the Workshop. But I don't think . . ."

"Does it mean working with kids?" Roxie asked. "Because I like kids, but they don't always like me. Sometimes they think I'm a little scary. I don't know why. I mean, sure I get upset sometimes, but I'm basically a nice person."

"Yes, you are," Sabrina assured her. "The best."

"So is the job something like yours?" Roxie asked her.

"No, this is strictly dealing with grown-ups. It's taking photo orders."

"Sounds great," Roxie said excitedly.

Sabrina gulped. She knew Roxie wouldn't be happy at Santa's Workshop. She tried to talk her out of applying for the position. "But they play Christmas music all day, and you know how you hate carols."

"I can deal with it," Roxie insisted.

"And everybody's jolly over there. You'd find it so annoying."

"Hey, I've lived with you for two years, haven't I? I can get used to jolly people."

"Roxie, I don't think this job's for you," Sabrina said helplessly.

Roxie leaned over the table and looked menacingly into Sabrina's eyes. "Look, I would have been happy with a typical King family Christmas—a take-out dinner, a box of Ring Dings, and then a joyful evening of throwing things at the Yule log on TV. But no. You had other ideas. Sabrina, this whole Secret Santa thing was your idea. Now I need money to buy a gift. I think you owe me this much."

A few minutes later, Sabrina returned to work with Roxie in tow. "Hey, Stan," she greeted the photographer. "I want you to meet my roommate Roxie King. She's looking for a job."

"What a coincidence." Stan smiled. "I'm looking for an employee. And if you're half as excited by the holidays as Sabrina is, you'll be perfect for our little Santa's Workshop family."

"Half as excited doesn't even begin to describe it," Roxie assured Stan. She forced a holiday smile to her lips. For a moment she looked almost cheerful.

"When can you start?" Stan asked her.

"How does tomorrow sound?" Roxie asked.

"Great!" Stan exclaimed. "You see that woman in the red hat?"

Roxie looked around. There were at least twenty people wearing red Santa hats. "Which one?"

"The one behind the table," Stan said. "Her name's Sarah. She'll give you some forms to fill out and show you what to do. You can start first thing."

"Great," Roxie said. "Um, what time is first thing?"

"Nine o'clock," Stan said. "We start bright and early at Santa's Workshop."

Sabrina gulped. Roxie was not a morning person.

But surprisingly, Roxie seemed fine with that. "I'll come in with my roommate here," she told him, pointing to Sabrina. "She'll make sure I wake up. You should hear her. She's so noisy in the morning. It's like an elephant is in the room!"

Sabrina scowled as Roxie and Stan shared a laugh. Stan turned to her. "Turn that frown upside down, Sabrina," he said. "We don't have any sour-pusses in Santa's Workshop."

Sabrina forced a smile to her lips, but glared at Roxie. Roxie just kept her holiday grin plastered to her face.

As Roxie walked off to meet with Sarah, Sabrina got a sick feeling in the pit of her stomach. Somehow she knew that having Roxie working in Santa's Workshop was a huge mistake.

Chapter 5

☆

☆

Roxie's first day of work started off uneventfully. Sure, Sabrina practically had to pull her out of bed by her hair, but hey, almost every morning started out that way. And of course, Roxie complained about the cold, the cost of Christmas trees, and the amount of gas that the SUVs in the mall parking lot were guzzling, but again, that wasn't unusual. Roxie was just being Roxie.

Sabrina just hoped that Roxie would become someone else while she was at work. For an instant, Sabrina was tempted to zap some holiday spirit into Roxie's Scrooge-like persona. But she was afraid Roxie might get stuck that way, and the truth was, there was something charming about the real Roxie.

"Good morning, girls!" Stan greeted Sabrina and Roxie as they wandered into Santa's Workshop just before nine. Already a line of children had formed near Santa's throne and Christmas carols were blaring from the loudspeakers throughout the Workshop.

"Hi," Sabrina greeted the photographer with a big smile. "Looks like another busy day here at the North Pole."

Roxie seemed confused. "The North Pole?"

"Yeah," Sabrina told her. "The North Pole. Where Santa lives."

"Oh yeah, right," Roxie replied. "We're supposed to act like Santa's a real guy. Do you really think that's a good thing to do?"

Sabrina and Stan both stared at Roxie.

"Shhh . . . ," Stan warned her. "The kids will hear you."

"Well, don't you think they should learn the truth early? Why lie to kids? We all know there's no Santa, and we're okay, aren't we?" Roxie asked.

Sabrina didn't reply. After all, she did know the truth about Santa. And the truth wasn't anything like what Roxie thought.

"Let's leave the life lessons to the parents," Stan told Roxie. "We're just here to sell photographs."

There was a loud excited gasp as Barney the mall Santa took his seat on the throne. The kids began pointing and jumping up and down excitedly. "Okay, folks," Stan called out to his staff. "Let's make the magic happen!"

Sabrina put on her elf hat and walked over toward the line of children. The first child in line was a baby who couldn't have been more than six months old. Her mother, a blond-haired woman with a nervous pinched-in expression on her face, handed the child to Sabrina.

"Please make sure you photograph her with her face slightly facing left. It's her best side," the mother told Sabrina.

Sabrina took the child in her arms. "Well, I guess she's not going to have a lot to say to Santa," Sabrina joked.

The mother glared at Sabrina. "She's not scheduled to actually speak for another three months. Although my Katherine *is* particularly advanced. She rolled over just before she turned three months. And just yesterday she pointed to the neighbor's dog and said, "A-roo."

"A genius," Sabrina laughed.

"Exactly," the woman agreed, completely missing the sarcasm in Sabrina's voice. "We're considering Harvard or Yale."

"Colleges?" Sabrina sounded suprised.

"You can never start thinking about these things too early."

Sabrina carried the baby up toward Santa and placed her on his lap. The baby looked up at the old man with the big white beard, and spit up on his jacket.

As Sabrina rushed over to get something to clean up the mess, she overheard the baby's mother say to the man behind her, "Look what my angel just did. It's like modern art."

Roxie's morning seemed to be going better than Sabrina's. Sarah, the woman in charge at the payment table, had given her a simple task, just to get her warmed up and acclimated to the work. Roxie's job was to make sure that the photo requests were all filled out correctly and accompanied by a check or credit card payment. The photos would be mailed out later. It wasn't hard work.

"How's it going?" Sabrina asked as she walked past the payment counter to get some more wipes—this time to clean up a wet stain left on Santa's lap by a leaky diaper.

"Not bad," Roxie said. "It's pretty easy. The hardest part is listening to those endless Christmas carols. Can't Stan play something else for a change?"

"Roxie, it's Christmas. You have to play holiday music."

Roxie nodded. "I guess."

Just then, Sarah walked over to where the girls were chatting. "Roxie, can you do me a favor?" she asked sweetly. "I need to go on a break. Could you take my place?"

"Sure," Roxie replied. "What do I need to do?"

"All you have to do is tell the parents about the different photo packages we offer. It's all on the sheet. Now, lots of them are going to try to go for the cheapest package—one free five-by-seven and a sheet of wallet-sized shots. But I want you to convince them to go for a bigger deal—maybe holiday cards and an eight-by-ten glossy as well. It's not hard—they all think their kids look like models anyway."

Sabrina braced herself. She was sure Roxie was going to have a big argument for Sarah—something about how awful it was to convince people to buy something they didn't need.

But suprisingly, Roxie just smiled. "Go take your break. I can handle it."

Sabrina looked at Roxie with surprise, but her roommate didn't return her glance. Instead, Roxie turned to the next couple in the photo-order line, forced herself to smile at their child, and said, "Now, what type of package did you have in mind?"

Sabrina was surprised, but happy. Maybe Roxie would do just fine taking photo orders. She felt herself relax as she went back to Santa and the never-ending line of children waiting to sit on his lap.

But before she could take the next little tot over to St. Nick, she heard Roxie's voice exploding over the music in Santa's Workshop.

"Oh, I can't. I just can't be this big of a hypocrite," Roxie moaned. "You don't need a big eight-by-ten photograph of your kid and some Santa wannabe. It's just another example of the commercialization of Christmas. Isn't it enough that you have the warm memory of little Susie here sitting on the guy's lap?"

"Her name is Haley," the flabbergasted mother muttered.

"Whatever," Roxie said. "You're missing the point. The thing is, Christmas isn't about getting presents or buying gifts, or that old guy over there pretending to be Santa Claus."

At that, little Haley began to bawl. "That's not Santa?" she cried out. "But he said he was Santa. Does that mean I'm not getting a puppy for Christmas?"

Now it was time for Haley's mother to get upset. "He promised you a puppy?" she demanded. "He had no right to . . ."

Haley's mother didn't have a chance to finish her sentence. At that moment, both Stan and Sarah came rushing over to the table.

"Roxie, please come with me," Stan said.

As Stan and Roxie walked away, Sarah took a seat behind the table. She smiled at Haley and her parents. "I'm sure Santa didn't promise you a puppy, did he Haley?"

"Well, not exactly," Haley admitted. "He said good girls get nice gifts, and I thought a puppy would be nice."

Sarah smiled up at Haley's mom. "Our Santa has been told not to make any promises," she assured the frustrated parents. "Now, let me help you and take your order."

"No, thank you," Haley's father remarked. "That young woman was right. Christmas isn't about cards and photos. It's about faith and joy. Today my daughter lost some of her faith, and she's definitely not experiencing joy. I'd like to forget we ever came here."

Haley and her parents stormed off.

A few moments later, Roxie appeared at Sabrina's side. "What happened?" Sabrina asked her.

"He told me to leave the workshop right away," Roxie said. "And get this. He said he wouldn't even pay me for the work I did this morning. Can you imagine? Talk about Scrooge."

"Sabrina, we have guests in the Workshop," Stan said sternly, pointing to the long line of children.

"You'd better get back to work, before he makes you turn in your hat," Roxie suggested. "I'll see you at home."

Chapter 6

By the time Sabrina got home that night, all she wanted was a hot bath. Her feet hurt and her head was pounding, she had chewing gum in her hair, and she smelled like a combination of baby spit up and sweat. She just wanted to be alone.

But Salem had other ideas. The cat had been at Sabrina's college house for quite a while, waiting to talk to her about his big kitty dilemma.

"Well, it's about time," Salem hissed as Sabrina walked into the house. "I've been waiting for you."

"Shhh," Sabrina warned him. "They'll hear you." The last thing Sabrina needed was her roommates knowing she had a talking cat. She was too tired to come up with an explanation they'd believe.

"There's no one here," Salem told her. "They all went out hours ago. It's just you and me."

Sabrina raised her finger and pointed it toward Salem. "Correction," she said, "it's just me. You're leaving."

"Wait!" Salem shouted before Sabrina could zap him back to Hilda and Zelda's. "I need your advice," he admitted, looking at her with big, pitiful yellow eyes.

Sabrina sighed and lowered her finger. She hated it when Salem looked at her like that. It made it impossible for her to tell him to get lost. "What?" she huffed as she plopped onto the couch and put her feet up on the coffee table.

"Do you think you could sound a little more synpathetic?" Salem asked her.

"No," Sabrina replied bluntly.

Salem sighed loudly, but he refused to let Sabrina's lack of enthusiasm keep him from talking. "I made it past the first cut in the Macho Male Favorite Familiars Calendar Contest. I'm in the running for Mr. April. It's not Mr. July, but it'll do."

Sabrina sat up, surprised. She'd seen Salem in that Speedo. He didn't even look like a runner-up to her. "That doesn't sound like a problem," she told the cat.

"I haven't gotten to the problem part yet," Salem informed her.

Sabrina kicked off her shoes. "Can you get to the part where you need my advice? I've had a long day."

Seeing the exhausted expression on Sabrina's face, Salem decided to cut to the chase. "The problem is my competition."

"Who's that?"

"Alexander Constantine," Salem hissed through clenched teeth.

"Who's he?"

Salem seemed surprised that Sabrina didn't recognize the name. "Alexander Constantine is my nemesis. He's the one who turned me in to the Witches Council. He's the reason I'm the cat I am today."

Sabrina seemed confused. "Is Alexander Constantine a familiar as well?"

Salem nodded. "A familiar of the worst kind. He's not just a cat, he's a copy cat. The Witches Council turned him into a tabby after he was caught trying to invade Europe."

"You mean . . . ," Sabrina began.

"That's right. After he turned me in to the Witches Council, Alexander tried to take over the world himself. Luckily he was caught in time. I'm telling you, Sabrina, the world would have been in trouble if his plan had succeeded. Alexander is ruthless."

"As opposed to you, who would have been a kind, benevolent king of the world?" Sabrina interjected sarcastically.

"Of course," Salem said. "I'm kind and fair and well loved."

"Not to mention modest," Sabrina joked. "I still don't see what the big deal is."

"The big deal is that Alexander the Not So Great is determined to win this contest. He'll stop at nothing to prove that he's more attractive than I am."

"Well, you'll have to compete like the kind, fair, well-loved cat you are," Sabrina told him.

Salem frowned. "That'll never work. You can't fight a cat like Alexander with fairness. I'll have to pull out all the stops."

Sabrina looked nervous. "What does that mean?"

"Nobody knows better than I do what kind of a man women like," Salem boasted.

"Oh really."

"Women like men who are brave, exciting, and full of danger."

"We do?"

Salem nodded, and hopped off the couch. "Thanks, Sabrina. You were a big help."

"I was?" Sabrina asked.

"Not really," Salem laughed as he leaped through the window and headed for home. "But I've got an idea."

Sitting alone in her house, Sabrina thought about what Salem had just said. She'd never seen her cat seem so threatened by anyone before. There was no telling what he would do.

But Sabrina didn't feel like worrying about Salem right now. She had bigger problems. Like how to get chewing gum out of her hair.

Sabrina didn't feel any better when she woke up the next morning. At least her hair wasn't still sticky with gum. (A little peanut butter had done the trick.) But she was still tired and cranky and decidedly lacking in Christmas spirit. It was kind of ironic. She'd come up with the Secret Santa Christmas gift exchange to put her roommates in the Christmas mood. But working to earn more money for a gift for Miles, on top of the other presents she still wanted to buy, had pretty much made the holiday a chore for Sabrina.

"Funny, I always thought working at Santa's Workshop would be fun," Sabrina said to herself. "Whenever we visited, the elves all seemed so jolly. But if the pressure at the real North Pole is anything like at the mall, those elves should ask for a bigger cut of the profits."

Sabrina scowled. It was Christmastime, and she was thinking about profits instead of sugar cookies and the *Nutcracker Suite*. What was happening to her?

Sabrina rolled out of bed and got dressed, taking extra care not to wake Roxie. Her roommate had had a rough enough time yesterday, and Sabrina figured the best gift she could give her was a good night's sleep before she had to go back out and pound the pavement for a new job.

As soon as she was completely dressed in her elf costume, Sabrina walked out into the living room. She discovered her roommate Morgan pouring through catalogs and typing something into the computer.

"Morning, Morgan," Sabrina murmured as she poured herself a much-needed cup of coffee.

"Oh good, Sabrina. You're just the person I wanted to talk to. I have a Christmas question for you."

Sabrina brightened. "Sure, Morgan. What do you want to know—the best place to get cute ornaments, or maybe what shelters need help serving the homeless on Christmas day?"

Morgan shook her head. "No. I just want your opinion. Which do you think I should add to my Christmas wish list—the superdeluxe hair-straightening kit or the complete home pedicure and foot Jacuzzi system I just found in this catalog?"

Sabrina rolled her eyes. Leave it to Morgan to completely miss the true meaning of Christmas. "Gee, Morgan, why not get both?" Sabrina replied sarcastically.

But Sabrina's tone was lost on Morgan. "You're right!" the redhead exclaimed. "Why not? And while I'm at it, maybe I should put the home facial center on my list as well." She turned to look Sabrina in the eye. "Do you think it's tacky to register for Christmas presents? I mean, it does save the hassle of having to return things I don't want."

Sabrina frowned. Sure, she'd heard of brides who registered for gifts at stores. That way, all the guests had to do was go to the store, pick out a gift from the bride's list, and order it as a wedding present.

But a *Christmas* registry? Sabrina had never heard of that. Besides, part of the fun of Christmas shopping was trying to figure out what your friends and family would want. It took creativity. And it was definitely more fun being surprised on Christmas morning than just getting something you'd already picked out. No, Sabrina didn't think a Christmas registry was a good idea at all—especially since Morgan had very expensive taste.

"Morgan, I'm not sure—," Sabrina began. But before she could get a word out, Miles appeared in the living room. His shirt was untucked, and the top button of his jeans was open.

"I can't believe this!" Miles moaned.

"What's wrong?" Sabrina asked him.

"I can' t button my pants. My mother's done nothing but send me Hanukkah care packages for the past eight days. I've eaten tons of fried potato pancakes, fried jelly donuts, and chocolate coins!" Miles plopped himself down on a kitchen chair. *Bam!* The chair collapsed beneath him.

"Ooh, Miles," Morgan said. Her face registered total disgust. "You have a huge zit on your chin. You shouldn't have eaten chocolate and fried food all in one week!"

"I hate the holidays!" Miles moaned as he ran into his room for a look in the mirror.

"Morgan, that was mean," Sabrina scolded. "It wasn't that big of a zit."

"Are you kidding?" Morgan replied. "It looked like a volcano erupting. His face needs a good cleansing." Suddenly her face turned white. "You don't think he's going to ask to borrow my skin-care supplies, do you?"

Sabrina shook her head. "I think he's more the Band-Aid on the chin type."

Morgan giggled. "That never works. Everyone always knows what you're hiding under there."

Sabrina took another sip of coffee.

"Maybe his Secret Santa should get him some sessions with a trainer . . . or a good dermatologist," Morgan mused as she poured through more catalogs.

His Secret Santa!

Sabrina glanced at the clock. Uh oh. If she didn't get moving, Miles wasn't going to have any gift from his Secret Santa. Stan wanted his employees at Santa's Workshop on time. Quickly Sabrina dashed out the door and headed for the mall.

"Okay, who's next?" Sabrina asked as she led one child out of Santa's Workshop and reached out her hand for the next customer. But the three-year-old boy at the front of the line didn't take Sabrina's hand. Instead he turned to his mother. "Don't wanna," he said.

"Billy, go with the nice elf," his mother urged. "Tell Santa what you want for Christmas."

"You can't make me!" Billy snapped. He stuck his tongue out at Sabrina.

Sabrina sighed. This morning was not going well at all. She'd had two leaky diaper emergencies, one little girl who had stuck her finger up her nose for her picture, and a boy who had pulled on Barney's beard really hard to see if it was real. Unfortunately for Barney, it was.

And now here was Billy, refusing to take a picture with Santa.

"Uh, Sabrina, there are a lot of kids waiting," Stan called out from his place behind the camera. "Let's keep it moving."

Sabrina nodded. "Come on, Billy. He's a really nice guy," she urged as she took his hand in hers.

"He's scawy," Billy mumbled.

"He's not scary. He's Santa," Sabrina told him.

Billy looked up at his mother. "He's a stwanger. You told me not to talk to stwangers," he tried.

"It's okay to talk to Santa," Billy's mother assured him.

But that wasn't enough to placate the boy. "WAAAAHHHHHH!" Billy began to wail at the top of his lungs.

At first everyone in the workshop grew silent. All eyes turned to Billy. Then total bedlam broke out. Before Billy's sudden tantrum, the kids in line all seemed happy and excited. Now they seemed frightened. Some began to whimper. A few tried to pull away, and a few others started to have tantrums. It was as though Billy's behavior was contagious.

Sabrina had to do something . . . and fast! Without thinking, she turned her back to Billy and the other kids in line. She quickly scanned the mall to make sure no one was looking at her and zapped a small box into her hands. Then she spun around.

"Congratulations!" she told Billy. "You're the tenth child today to sit on Santa's lap. You get this prize—if you go to Santa and smile."

That was all it took. Billy's big brown eyes lit up as he took the box from Sabrina's hands. He walked happily up to the mall Santa, hopped on his lap, and smiled for Stan's camera.

As Billy and his mother headed over toward Sarah's station to order their photos, Sabrina got a sick feeling in the pit of her stomach. Giving Billy that gift might have been a mistake. After all, a zapped gift could come with a lot of Other Realm baggage. She held her breath as Billy ripped the wrapping from the box, opened the package, and pulled out a toy truck.

Billy took the blue-and-white truck in his hands and sat down on the floor. He moved the truck forward and backward. Sabrina watched anxiously, waiting for something to go wrong. But nothing did. The truck was simply a truck. No magic involved.

Sabrina grinned as she watched Billy play with his new toy. He seemed happy. His mother seemed relieved. And Sabrina still had her job.

Sometimes things did work out just the way you planned them.

Sabrina returned to work with a new sense of joy. Her aunts were always telling her to take responsibility and learn to solve her own problems. That was what she had just done.

But Sabrina hadn't completely solved her problems.

"Come on, let's go meet Santa," Sabrina told the next girl in line.

"Where's my present?" the girl demanded.

"You'll get your presents on Christmas morning," Sabrina reminded her gently. "Now let's go tell Santa what you want. Maybe he'll be able to bring it to you when he and his reindeer take that big ride through the sky on Christmas Eve."

"But that little boy got a present. I want one, too!" She stamped her foot really hard—right onto Sabrina's elf shoe.

"Ow!" Sabrina shouted, grabbing her foot.

"Sabrina, let's keep it going!" Stan reminded her.

Sabrina didn't know what to do. She couldn't just zap up another gift right here in front of everyone. But without it, this little girl wasn't going to move.

"My Madison has a point," the little girl's father said. He looked at Sabrina. "I'm a lawyer. I could sue you for favoritism."

Sabrina wasn't sure he could actually do that. Still, she didn't want to wait to find out. "But Billy won his truck by being the tenth child in line," Sabrina began to explain.

"I don't see a sign saying that the tenth child wins

a prize," Madison's lawyer-father began. "If I had, I would have made certain that Madison was tenth." He smiled at his daughter. "My little girl likes it when she's the winner. I like it when my little girl is happy."

Sabrina sighed. Little Madison hadn't fallen far from the tree.

"Um . . . well . . . ," Sabrina stammered, stalling until she could come up with an excuse. "I'll tell you what. If Madison sits on Santa's lap, I'll see what I can do. Maybe I can find a balloon or something."

"That won't do at all!" Madison's father bellowed. "We require a gift equal to or more expensive than the gift the boy got."

"Sabrina!" Stan called again. He sounded angry.

"Just go in the chair," Sabrina assured Madison. "I'll find you something special."

"That's better!" Madison and her father said at the same time.

As Madison hopped onto Santa's lap, Sabrina walked behind the big throne. For a moment, she considered going off to buy Madison a doll at the local toy store. But she knew that wasn't going to solve anything. For starters, she didn't have any money at the moment. She wasn't going to be paid until the end of the week. And she needed *that* money to do her Christmas shopping.

Sabrina had no choice. She waved her finger and zapped up a gift for Madison.

By the time Sabrina returned to Santa's side, Madison was happily rattling off something that sounded more like a toy store catalog than a child's Christmas wish list.

"Okay, Madison," Sabrina urged. "I've got your gift. Now smile for the camera."

"But I still have three pages of my wish list left," Madison told her. She held up a thick stack of papers.

"Well, Santa has some good ideas," Sabrina assured her. "Now smile and you'll get what's in the box."

Madison did as she was told. As soon as the flash went off, Madison leaped off of Santa's lap and held out her hands. "Gimme!" she demanded.

Sabrina gave the little girl the box and watched anxiously as she opened the package and pulled out a small baby doll. Sabrina waited for the doll to come to life, or speak, or have some other Other Realm action. But nothing happened. The doll just lay there, like any regular toy.

Madison held the doll tight. "You're my baby," she whispered. Then she turned to Sabrina. "Santa *is* magical!" she said, her eyes suddenly lighting up. "I wished for a baby doll for Christmas, and look what was in my box. I've never had a baby doll before."

Sabrina looked at Madison with surprise. Madison was at least five years old. Surely her parents had bought her a doll at some point.

Or maybe not.

"I would have preferred an educational toy," Madison's father told Sabrina. "Something that would have honed her mind and made her think. Those are the kinds of gifts we buy for our daughter. What can she learn from a doll?"

Madison's father's words meant nothing to Sabrina. She was busy watching the little girl play with her doll. Madison cradled the doll in her arms and began to sing a lullaby. Then she kissed it gently on the forehead and smiled with a mother's pride. It was obvious that at that moment, Madison wasn't thinking with her mind—she was thinking with her heart. Having a doll filled Madison with joy. Suddenly the little girl seemed sweet and innocent, like a five-year-old should be. She loved her doll, and she loved Santa.

Madison looked up at Sabrina. "What's your name?" she asked.

"Sabrina."

"That's my baby's name, too!" Madison exclaimed. "I just decided."

"I'm flattered," Sabrina replied sincerely.

In one swift motion, Madison leaped up and landed in Sabrina's arms. She hugged her tight. "Thank you!" Madison whispered into Sabrina's ear. "Thank you for my baby."

"Thank *you*," Sabrina whispered back to her.

"But I didn't give you anything," Madison replied.

Sabrina smiled at the little girl. "Oh, yes, you did," she assured her. "You gave Christmas back to me."

Chapter 7

Salem wasn't depending on magic to reach his goals. Of course if he could have, he would have. Salem was not above taking the easy way out. But seeing as he didn't have his magic powers any more, he was left to using brain power to get what he wanted.

Salem had devised a great plan for winning the calendar competition. He was going to show the judges how brave, macho, and deserving he was. The only way to do that was to try his hand at some Xtreme sports.

Salem had been doing his research. He knew there were plenty of Xtreme sports Web sites posted. They featured sports like snowboarding, BMX biking, MotoX, skateboarding, and rock climbing. Xtreme sports were not for the faint of heart. But the people who competed in them were worshipped by millions. And that's exactly what Salem hoped to be. He figured that if the judges could see him participating in such elite competitions, they'd be sure to choose him over Alexander Constantine as Mr. April.

Which is why, at that very moment, Salem was standing at the top of a mountain at an Other Realm ski resort and sports center, with nothing but a plastic snowboard separating him from a steep slope of snow.

"Now, all you have to do is take my picture while I'm in the air," Salem told his pal, Lenny. Salem had brought Lenny to the ski lodge as his personal photographer.

Lenny tried to nod, but his head seemed frozen.

"What's wrong with you?" Salem asked.

"I'm a lizard," Lenny reminded him. "Cold blooded, remember? I'm not supposed to be out in the snow."

Salem nodded. Lenny had it rough. About two hundred years ago he'd been caught planning a coup to take over the Witches Council. They didn't take that very well. In fact, they'd been a lot angrier at Lenny than they'd been at Salem. They'd sentenced

Lenny to 350 years as a lizard. That was a long time to have to snack on crickets and cockroaches.

"Tell me again what I'm getting out of this?" Lenny asked through chattering teeth.

"You'll be able to say that you're part of an intimate circle of friends of a famous model," Salem assured him. "That's a great line to use when you're looking for a date."

Lenny shivered. "I guess." He looked at the steep ski trail before him. "Are you sure you want to go on the expert trail? I mean, maybe you should start with something simpler, like the bunny slope, and work up to this."

Salem shook his head. "First of all, those bunnies hip-hopping down that trail make it impossible to navigate. Second of all, it costs too much to take fake pictures of this stuff. Besides, I am a natural athlete."

"But—"

"No buts about it," Salem told Lenny. "Now, make sure you get a good shot of me as I fly through the air on the snowboard. That's really impressive."

"Are you sure this is a good idea?" Lenny asked.

Salem couldn't believe how clueless the lizard

was. "Lenny, this calendar's aimed at women. Women love Xtreme sportsmen."

"How do you know that?" the lizard asked.

"I just know," Salem assured him. "I understand women. I know what they want in a man."

"You're not a man," Lenny reminded him. "You're a cat."

Salem sighed. "So I've been told. Now point that camera and get ready for a little macho magic."

Salem pulled his snow goggles over his eyes and prepared to take the snowboard down the hill. But before he could push off, a brown, black, and white tabby cat appeared beside him.

"Hello, Saberhagen," the cat purred.

"Alexander the Not So Great," Salem replied. "What are you doing here?"

"I could ask you the same thing."

"I'm snowboarding. It's one of my hobbies," Salem replied. "I'm a daredevil kind of guy."

"Since when?"

"Since . . . well . . ." Salem wasn't sure how to answer that one. He actually had never snowboarded or done any Xtreme sport before. But he wasn't about to admit that to his arch rival. "Look, I'd love to stay and catch up, but I'm about to take this hill," Salem said with false bravado.

"Right beside you," Alexander replied, pulling on his snow goggles. *"Every step of the way."*

With that, the two cats took off down the mountain at top speed. From the minute they began moving, it was obvious that neither feline had the faintest idea how to snowboard. Within seconds, they'd both lost control, tumbling through the snow.

"AAAHHHH!" Salem shouted as his little body picked up speed.

"AAAAAHHH!" Alexander seconded.

"AAAAAHHHHHH!" Salem shouted again, making sure his scream was louder and longer than Alexander's.

The cats rolled down the mountain, picking up snow as they went. Before long they both looked like giant snowballs. They didn't stop rolling until they crashed into a huge tree.

Salem lay there in the snow for a minute, gathering his wits about him. Slowly he sat up and rubbed his head with his paw. He had a big lump where he'd collided with the tree. And his limbs were frozen.

Lenny came slithering over. "Say cheese!" he said, snapping away with the camera."

"Not now," Salem moaned.

"Okay," Lenny agreed. "I got plenty of shots anyway."

"Ooooh, my aching head," Salem moaned.

"Don't try to move," Lenny urged. "They're sending a rescue squad." The lizard looked farther down the mountain. "Oh good, here they come now."

"How many men are there?" Salem asked him.

"Oh, there are no men," Lenny said. "They've sent a dog team to rescue you."

"Dogs?" Salem groaned. "I'm being rescued by dogs? Could this get any more humiliating?"

Within seconds two giant, furry dogs appeared on the scene. Each dog lifted a cat in his mouth. Salem tried to hide his face with his front paw. If anyone he knew saw him in the mouth of a dog . . . Salem shuddered at the thought of it.

As the animals moved down the mountain, Alexander licked at a big cut on his leg. "Salem, now that you're injured, I guess you'll be giving up the contest," he told Salem.

"Why would I do that?" Salem replied, sounding very determined. "Are you?"

"Absolutely not," Alexander said, sounding equally determined. "You'll never beat me, Salem Saberhagen."

Salem stood up. "Oh yes, I will," he assured the other cat.

As they reached the bottom of the mountain, the Saint Bernard dropped Salem off near the ski lodge.

"Thanks," Salem said begrudgingly. Then he turned to Lenny. "Come on, we have more photos to shoot."

"Where are you going?" Alexander asked him.

"Wouldn't you like to know," Salem replied as he limped off toward the ski lodge.

An hour later Salem and Lenny found themselves in a warmer environment—at an indoor skateboarding ramp.

"Are you sure you want to do this?" Lenny asked. "I don't think it's as easy as it looks."

"How hard can it be?" Salem retorted. "Kids can do it."

"Don't you think you should be wearing some of the protective gear the other skateboarders are wearing?" Lenny wondered

"Oh, yeah," Salem hissed sarcastically. "I'd look real macho in a helmet and pads. No, I'm not wearing that stuff. Besides, I won't be here long. I'm just going up and down the ramp while you snap shots. What could happen?"

"My thoughts exactly," Alexander Constantine agreed as he snuck up behind Salem.

"Are you following me?" Salem demanded.

"I thought you were following me."

"I was here first," Salem insisted.

"Well, I'll be the last one standing," Alexander assured him.

"That sounds like a dare," Salem said.

"Take it as you will," Alexander replied.

Salem wasn't one to back down from a dare. He leaped onto his kitty-sized skateboard and started down the ramp. The momentum carried him up the other side of the ramp, exactly as it was supposed to. Salem grinned a Cheshire cat smile. This was obviously his sport.

"Whoo hoo look at me!" he shouted out.

"No, look at me!" Alexander countered.

Unfortunately neither cat was looking where he was going. *Bonk!* They collided right into each other.

"Ow!" Salem moaned as he fell from his skateboard.

"Why didn't you watch where you were going?" Alexander snapped at Salem.

"Me?" Salem replied. "You're the one who got in my way!"

"I did not," Alexander told him. "I totally had the right of way."

"Fellas, don't argue over this," Lenny interrupted. "I got the whole thing on film. We can figure out whose fault this was as soon as I get these pictures developed. Now say cheese," he said as he snapped a few more shots.

Salem was in too much pain to smile at Lenny's camera. Instead, the injured cat grabbed his swollen back paw and looked longingly toward the first aid center. "Medic!" he cried out.

Chapter 8

While Salem was busy turning Xtreme sports into Xtreme pain, Sabrina was happily enjoying bringing Christmas joy into the lives of the tots that were visiting Santa's Workshop that afternoon. Ever since Madison had named her doll after Sabrina and given her that big hug, the job no longer seemed difficult. Instead, Sabrina had relaxed enough to make the experience fun. She no longer had to deal with any crying children. In fact, the only time kids cried at Santa's Workshop was when Sabrina was on her break and one of the other elves took over. It seemed all the kids wanted to meet the "Toy Lady." Sabrina didn't know which child had given her that nickname, but she kind of liked it.

She also deserved it. Sabrina had spent a good part of her day zapping up toys for the kids who were waiting to see Santa. All of her fears about using magic to make toys for the kids had disappeared. By noon Sabrina had zapped up dozens of toys for crying children, and not one of those toys appeared to have a single bit of Other Realm magic in them. It seemed that Christmas toys were exempt from the weirdness that accompanied Sabrina's usual forays into bringing magic to the Mortal Realm. So Sabrina felt no apprehension at all about zapping up rattles or plastic teething rings for crying babies. For the older children, she'd come up with a vast selection of dolls, baseballs, toy trucks, and miniature sports cars all specially designed to make them smile for the camera.

Sabrina's technique for getting the kids to pose for the pefect Christmas picture hadn't escaped Stan's notice. He was well aware that Sabrina had built up his business. After all, the bigger the smile on the child's face, the more likely the parents were to buy lots and lots of copies of Stan's photographs. As Sabrina took a lunch break, Stan pulled her aside. "That idea about giving the kids toys was brilliant, Sabrina. It showed real initiative," he complimented her. "But I hope you weren't counting on me paying you back for them. I mean I'd love to be able to do that, but this is just a small business. I don't have a budget for toys. And it was your idea, after all."

Sabrina nodded. She'd never expected to be compensated for the gifts. "That's okay, Stan," she assured her boss. "I have a way of getting the toys very cheaply. It's payment enough to see those kids so happy."

Stan smiled at her. "You're just the kind of elf we like around here," he told Sabrina. "Say, how do you feel about chickens?"

"Chickens?" Sabrina asked.

"At Easter time. We'll need some chickens to help Mr. Easter Bunny when we set up our springtime photo setting."

Sabrina's mind drifted back to her experience as the cow at Svenson's Cheese Emporium. "I'm not really good at barnyard animals," she told Stan.

Stan shrugged. "Okay, well, let me know if you change your mind."

"I will," Sabrina assured him. "I'm going to take my break now. I'll see you in half an hour."

Sabrina took off her elf hat and began walking toward the food court. She didn't get very far before she spotted Roxie sitting on a bench not far from Santa's Workshop. As soon as she spotted Sabrina,

Roxie slipped something small and black into her purse and tried to run off.

"Hey, Roxie!" Sabrina called out. "Wait up!"

Roxie kept walking. But Sabrina was faster. Within seconds she was next to her roommate.

"Sabrina!" Roxie exclaimed. "What a surprise."

"Surprise?" Sabrina asked. "I work here. You know that."

"I must have forgotten."

Sabrina studied Roxie's face. The girl was obviously up to something. The question was, what? "So, why are you at the mall?" she asked her.

"Can't a girl do a little shopping before Christmas?" Roxie asked.

"But you don't have any money," Sabrina reminded her.

"Oh yeah," Roxie said nervously. She glanced into a dress shop. "Say, isn't that Morgan?" she asked, changing the subject. "What do you think she's doing?"

Sabrina glanced into the store. Morgan was holding a pale pink dress up against her body and admiring herself in the mirror. "It looks like she's shopping for a dress. Which makes sense, since that *is* a boutique."

"Yeah," Roxie said. "She's probably buying herself another Christmas present."

"Probably," Sabrina agreed. "Nobody knows Morgan's taste better than Morgan."

Roxie looked at her wrist. "Wow! Look at the time!" she exclaimed. "I gotta go."

Sabrina watched curiously as her best friend ran off. Roxie sure was acting strange. How could she possibly have known what time it was? She hadn't been wearing a watch!

Sabrina, however, *was* wearing a watch. And it told her that her break would be over in less than twenty minutes. She didn't have time to wonder what Roxie was up to. She had to get something to eat.

"Did you at least get a good picture of me climbing on the rocks?" Salem asked Lenny. They were waiting in the emergency room of the Other Realm veterinary hospital. Salem was waiting to get a cat CAT scan of his injured head and limbs.

"You mean before you plummeted to the ground below?" Lenny replied.

Salem nodded. "Yeah. While I was still up there looking buff and brave."

Lenny shook his head. "No. I was busy changing the film. I did get some great shots of you falling, though. They're some of the best candid pictures I've ever taken. I'll tell you, buddy. You're a great subject. A first-class model!" He gave Salem a congratulatory slap on the back.

"OOOWWWWWW!" Salem screeched out in pain.

Lenny looked down sheepishly. "Sorry, pal."

"Never mind," Salem said. "What's taking those doctors so long? I've been waiting in this emergency room for a long time. I think I've gone through at least two of my nine lives."

Lenny laughed. "That's a good one, Salem," he said, giving him a congratulatory pat on the back.

"MEOWWWWWWWW!" Salem cried out in agony. "Oh . . . can't you ask them to take me for those X rays now?

"There's only one CAT scan machine. Alexander Constantine's using it," Lenny explained. "His ambulance beat yours here."

"And he'll be pointing that out for the next hundred years," Salem groused. "Well, it's better that he beat me here than in the calendar contest."

"Oh, there's *no* contest there," Lenny assured

Salem. "You're much more photogenic. When I took his picture after he fell off the rock wall, he looked completely smushed. You just looked stunned. Stunned photographs better than smushed any day."

"Thanks," Salem said unconvincingly.

"So are you feeling any better, buddy?" Lenny asked him.

"Not really," Salem replied. "I think the only thing that doesn't hurt right now is my tail."

Lenny nodded understandingly. "I'll go ask the nurse how much longer until you can get into that CAT scan room." He leaped down from his chair.

"YOWWWWWWW!" Salem cried out in pain.

"What's wrong?" Lenny asked him.

"Let's just say that now there's no part of my body that doesn't hurt!" Salem moaned as he pulled his tail out from under Lenny's feet.

Sabrina was tired when she came home from work that night. Her feet hurt, she smelled like a combination of candy and baby dribble, and her hair was a mess. But she was happy. She'd managed to bring a smile to the faces of so many children. And even though she'd used magic to whip up their surprise gifts, not one present had backfired on her. For once, no one had gotten hurt by one of Sabrina's spells. Everything had worked out exactly the way she'd hoped.

When Sabrina walked into the house, Miles was on the phone. "I guess purple would be good, unless you had some sort of red," she heard him say into the receiver. "Red," he repeated. "You know, like the Red Spot of Jupiter? Never mind. What color does the mud come in? Do I have to book early if I want a silver rocket ship?"

Sabrina looked at him curiously. The Red Spot of Jupiter? Colored mud? Rocket ship? The last time Sabrina had heard Miles talking like that, an unscrupulous con artist had tried to sell him a seat on the space shuttle. Sabrina hoped he wasn't falling for that again.

As soon as Miles spotted Sabrina, he slammed down the phone, not even waiting for a response from the person on the other end. Instead he looked up and smiled one of those fake smiles people give when they don't want someone to know what they're up to.

"Hi, Sabrina," he said quickly. "What a surprise. What are you doing here?"

"I live here," Sabrina reminded him.

"Yeah, of course you do. This is *your* house, too. Ha ha." Miles sounded very nervous. "Boy, have I gotten forgetful lately. What's my name? When's my birthday?" he joked.

Sabrina studied Miles's face. He was acting very strangely. And for Miles, that was saying something, since he was sort of strange to begin with. "So, what's new, Miles?" Sabrina asked.

"Not much. You?" Miles replied.

"You know, I saw Roxie at the mall today and—" Before Sabrina could finish her conversation with Miles, the phone rang. Miles seemed very relieved. He hurried to pick up the receiver. "Hello?" he said. "Oh. Yes, she's right here." He handed the phone to Sabrina. "It's your aunt Hilda."

"Hi, Aunt Hilda," Sabrina said as she took the phone from Miles.

"Hi yourself," Hilda said. "How are you? We haven't heard from you in a while."

"Well, I've been busy."

"Yes, I know," Hilda assured her. "You've been working at the Santa's Workshop in the mall."

"How did you know?" Sabrina asked.

"Oh, a little elf told me," Hilda replied. "I need you to come over, okay?"

"Can I come tomorrow?" Sabrina answered. "I'm kind of beat. I've been making kids smile all day."

"So I've heard," Hilda remarked.

"What do you mean?"

Hilda was firm. "Sabrina, you need to come home right now. It's an emergency."

Chapter 9

Sabrina didn't take the time to walk to her aunts' house. Instead she went outside, hid in the bushes behind her house, and used her magic to zap herself right over. Quickly she opened the door.

"Aunt Hilda, Aunt Zelda, I'm here. What's the big emer—" Sabrina stopped mid-sentence when she heard a cacophony come from the living room. "What's all that racket?" she asked.

Zelda jumped up and stopped Sabrina before she could walk all the way into the living room.

"Sabrina, please, we have guests," she whispered.

"Why are they screaming at each other?" Sabrina whispered back.

"They're pretty angry," Zelda explained. "They really couldn't afford to take time away from the North Pole, but—"

"The North Pole?" Sabrina asked excitedly. "Is Santa here?"

"Oh, yes," Zelda said. "He's here especially to see you."

Sabrina grinned broadly. "I'll bet he's here to congratulate me. Maybe even make me a deputy elf. He must have heard about the great job I'm doing with the kids in the mall."

"Oh, he's heard about it all right," Zelda assured Sabrina as she stepped aside and let her niece into the living room.

Sabrina entered the room. Santa and one of his elves were sitting on the couch. Sabrina's aunt Hilda was sitting in a big easy chair, as far away from the noise as possible. Zelda didn't seem to want to move away from the open door.

"There she is!" a small elf shouted as he leaped off the couch and pointed. "It's Sabrina. Let me at her!"

"Yep, it's me, Sabrina," she said proudly. She held out her hand. "And you would be . . . ?"

"Furious with you, you elf imposter!" Santa's elf declared.

"Now, Rufus, calm down," Santa said. "Let's give Sabrina a chance to defend herself."

"I say we put her on the lump of coal list right now," Rufus snapped. "It's all we have left anyhow."

Sabrina looked curiously at Rufus and Santa. "Coal?" she asked. "But that's what you leave in the stockings of kids who are naughty, not nice."

"Well, if the stocking fits . . . ," Rufus began.

"Rufus," Santa warned. He turned his gaze toward Sabrina. "You'll have to forgive Rufus. He's a very dedicated elf. He takes his job seriously."

"Being an elf is an honor," Rufus told Sabrina. "It isn't something we take lightly."

"I don't take it lightly either," Sabrina assured him. "I know I'm not a real elf, but I tried hard to do honor to your profession."

"Honor?!" Rufus demanded. He jumped up and down. "Is that what you call your behavior?"

Santa put a chubby hand on Rufus's shoulder. "Easy now," he urged the elf. "Fighting isn't going to solve this."

"Solve what?" Sabrina asked.

"We have a slight problem," Santa explained.

"Slight?" Rufus interrupted. "Disappointed children on Christmas Day is not a slight problem, boss. It's a public relations disaster! When word gets out that we weren't able to make our deliveries as promised, well . . ." The elf's face grew red with rage. "I don't know how we'll be able to fix this mess. We'll just have to let everyone know the whole thing is her fault." He turned his attention to Sabrina. "I'm warning you, young lady—when I get through with you, you're going to be public enemy number one in the eyes of the world's children. I won't let anyone give Santa's elves a bad name."

Now Sabrina was totally confused. "But kids love me!" she assured Rufus. "Just this afternoon I was with lots of children, and they were all hugging me, and kissing me, and calling me the Toy Lady. . . ."

"Ah, yes. The Toy Lady. That brings me to our problem," Santa interrupted. "You've been giving out toys all day."

"Yep," Sabrina said. "I'm filled with the spirit of giving."

"That's very nice, dear," Santa replied. "But you've been giving away toys that aren't yours to give."

"The toys aren't anybody's. I just zapped up a few Christmas presents," Sabrina explained.

"Oh, Sabrina, you didn't," Zelda moaned.

"Don't worry, Aunt Zelda, the toys weren't magic. They were just toys. No harm done."

"But there *was* harm done. A great deal of harm." Santa's old blue eyes misted over as he explained the problem. "You see, Sabrina, those weren't just any toys. Those were Christmas toys—made at the North Pole. You zapped toys away from our very carefully calculated stock."

Sabrina looked confused.

"There's a fixed number of toys that the elves make every year," Santa continued. There are only so many Christmas gifts for all the good little boys and girls in the world. It may have appeared as though the toys came out of thin air, but those toys you gave away actually came from my Workshop. They've been disappearing all day."

Sabrina gasped. "But I . . . I didn't mean to . . ."

Santa shrugged. "I'm sure you had only the best intentions." He pulled out a Palm Pilot and scanned the screen looking for Sabrina's name. "According to my records, you're basically a nice person."

"Is that your official naughty and nice list?" Sabrina asked. "I thought you kept that information in a big notebook."

"Oh, we're completely computer automated at the North Pole now," Santa told her. "We've got to move with the times."

"I guess," Sabrina agreed. "But that image of you with the book was so sweet. . . ."

"Tick tock. Time's a-wastin', thief," Rufus interrupted.

"I'm not a thief," Sabrina insisted.

"Maybe not," Santa agreed. "But we still have a big problem. We don't have enough toys to deliver on Christmas Eve. Some stockings are going to be left empty."

"And in case you've forgotten, Christmas Eve is tomorrow night," Rufus reminded Sabrina. "There's no time to fix this mess."

A look of panic and embarrassment came over Sabrina. "But I didn't know . . . ," she stammered.

"Sabrina," Zelda interrupted. "You must have known that you can't ever get something for nothing. There's a price to pay for everything."

"This is a disaster. I was expecting a lot of good stuff this year," Hilda said sadly. She folded her arms in front of her like an angry, disappointed child.

"I'm sorry," Sabrina apologized.

"Sorry isn't going to solve anything," Rufus told her.

"Are you sure you can't make enough toys before tomorrow night?" Sabrina begged Santa.

The old man shook his head. "The elves are all working very hard. But there just aren't enough of them. We'd need more elf power to fill the gap you've created."

"Speaking of which, I gotta get back, boss," Rufus told Santa. "I've been gone too long already. We need every elf we can get."

As soon as Santa and Rufus had left, Sabrina went up to her old room. She didn't feel like going back to her college house right away. There were too many people there. Sabrina needed to be alone so she could think.

Unfortunately Sabrina wasn't alone in her old room, either. Salem was already in there. He was curled up on her bed, nursing his wounds.

"Wow! What happened to you?" Sabrina asked him. "You look awful."

"I can't look any worse than I feel," Salem assured her.

Sabrina looked at the cat's bandaged tail, his swollen left eye, the shaved part of his back left paw where the doctor put in the stitches, and the lump on the side of his head. "How did you manage to get so hurt?" she asked him.

"There's a reason they call them Xtreme sports," Salem replied. "But never mind me. Why do you look like something the cat dragged in—if I had the strength to drag anything, that is."

Sabrina flopped down beside Salem on the bed and sighed. "I hate Christmas!" she declared.

"Since when?" Salem asked her.

"Since I ruined it," she replied.

"I don't have the energy to ask how," Salem told her. "I'm just going to assume it was another spell gone bad."

Sabrina nodded. "At least my roommates will be happy."

"Why?" Salem asked.

"They never had the Christmas spirit to begin with. This'll just prove that they were right," Sabrina moaned. "And you know how people love to be right."

Salem couldn't disagree with that. "Guess you can't fix things, huh?"

Sabrina shook her head. "Tomorrow's Christmas Eve. A lot of kids are going to be without gifts in their stockings, and I'm the one to blame. I'm about to go down in history as the world's most unpopular person."

"I thought you already had," Salem joked.

"Excuse me?"

"Wasn't that your nickname during high school?" Salem teased.

Sabrina scowled. It was just like Salem to kick her when she was down. Too bad those doctors hadn't wired his mouth shut while they were bandaging him up. "Very funny. At least I don't look like a used crash test dummy," she snapped back.

Salem nodded. No argument there. He did look completely beat up. But he was willing to take the pain. It was a small price to pay for the glory that would soon be his. "I'll admit that Xtreme sports were more Xtreme than I'd bargained for, but once Lenny develops those pictures of me in action, I'll be a legend! The Macho Male Favorite Familiars people will be all over me to be in their calendar. They might even want to do a whole Salem Saberhagen calendar. A different Salem photo for every month."

"Are you sure this is all worth it—just to get a few free Christmas gifts?" Sabrina asked him.

"Next year, when all my scars are healed and I'm busy spending my Christmas money on myself instead of on other people, you'll be very jealous."

Sabrina looked dubious.

"This year I'll tell them they got stiffed because you screwed things up," Salem said. "Hey! That's a great excuse. Thanks, Sabrina!"

Sabrina couldn't argue with Salem. He was right. She gasped. *The cat was right!* That wasn't possible. Salem was never right. Ooh! This Christmas was getting worse and worse.

Sabrina took a deep breath. There was no way she was going to let Christmas be ruined for a whole lot of kids. "Gotta go!" she said.

"Where?" Salem asked her.

Sabrina grinned. "I'm off to find some elves."

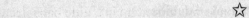

Chapter 10

"Hey, you guys! Anybody up?" Sabrina asked as she entered her college house.

No one answered. Sabrina looked around. The place was completely dark. No one had even bothered to turn on the Christmas tree lights or the dancing Santa in the window.

"What a bunch of humbugs!" Sabrina whispered to herself. Then she grinned slightly. All that was about to change. Sabrina had a plan. And if everything went the way she hoped, Santa would have his toys, and her friends would gain some Christmas spirit.

But first she had to make sure that everyone was fast asleep. The plan would only work if her friends were already happily immersed in dreamland. Quickly Sabrina rushed into her room. Sure enough,

Sabrina's roomie was curled up in a little ball, sleeping peacefully. Sabrina stifled a giggle. Roxie looked so sweet when she slept . . . but Sabrina would never dare tell her that.

Next Sabrina cracked open the door to Morgan's room. She gasped as she looked over toward the bed. At first glance, it looked as though a green-skinned monster had taken over Morgan's space. But as her eyes adjusted to the darkness, Sabrina realized that the monster in the bed was indeed Morgan—she was just wearing a thick, green night cream and a mask over her eyes.

Sabrina slipped out of Morgan's room and headed over toward Miles's bedroom. She pushed the door open a bit and peeked in. Miles, too, was fast asleep. He lay on his side cuddling a furry tribble from his Star Trek plush toy collection.

Thoughts began to race through Sabrina's mind as she walked out of Miles's room. She was certain that her plan would work. Her housemates all seemed to be peacefully involved in their own personal dreams—which would make it that much easier for Sabrina to explain what was about to happen to them.

But she'd better get moving if Santa was going to

make his deadline. Quickly Sabrina placed her feet firmly in the center of the living room. She began to chant:

"I've heard complaints from St. Nick and his elf.
I have no one to blame but myself.
There's no time to cry, scream, or yelp.
Santa needs a lot of help.
To come up with more trucks,
dolls, and spinning tops,
take us all to Santa's Workshop!"

Sabrina snapped her fingers, and in an instant, Roxie, Miles, and Morgan were all standing by her side—at the North Pole. Sabrina had zapped them all to the real Santa's Workshop.

Sabrina smiled as her eyes focused on the workshop. It had been a while since she and her aunts had visited the Clauses, but nothing had changed. The Workshop cottage was still beautiful. Shimmering snow blanketed the roof, and big, green pine trees lined the entranceway. Best of all, a picket fence made of real giant candy canes surrounded the house. On her last visit, Santa had let her eat part of the fence as a special treat. For a moment, Sabrina was tempted to break off a piece. But she thought better of it. Sabrina wasn't exactly on Santa's list of favorite witches at the moment. She didn't want to take anything else that didn't belong to her.

As a cold breeze blew through the pine trees, Sabrina began to shiver. "Darn," she complained as she wrapped her arms tightly around her chest. She'd forgotten to zap her parka to the North Pole with her.

Sabrina wasn't the only one who was freezing. Her friends were cold, too.

"Hey, who opened the window?" Morgan moaned sleepily. She had no idea where she was—after all, her eyes were still covered by her sleep mask.

But Roxie's eyes were wide open. She could plainly see the big wooden cottage in the snow. "Whoa, this is some dream," she exclaimed. "It's all so real."

"I know what you mean," Miles replied. "I swear I can smell candy canes."

"Yeah," Roxie replied. She lifted up one of her bare feet. It was cold and wet from the snow. "I think I'm getting frostbite."

"Let's get inside," Sabrina said as she led her roommates around to the back entrance of the Workshop.

"Hey, what are you doing in my dream?" Roxie asked her. She turned to Miles and Morgan. "Why are you here?"

Sabrina gulped. "Um . . . well . . . I read somewhere that people who've been living together for a long time can share dreams. It's some weird subconscious thing." She held her breath, waiting to see if her roommates would fall for such a bizarre explanation.

"I think I read that in one of my fashion magazines," Morgan agreed as she removed her sleep mask.

"I didn't think you read any of the articles in those magazines," Roxie said. "I thought you just looked at the pictures."

"Hmmm, you're right," Morgan agreed. "Oh well."

Since there didn't seem to be any more discussions about the dream state, Sabrina assumed her roommates had accepted her explanation. She continued to lead them around to the workshop. Along the way, they passed by the reindeer pen. Dasher, Dancer, Prancer, Vixen, Comet, Cupid, Donner, Blitzen, and Rudolph were all happily munching on oats and barley—loading up on carbohydrates for their marathon flight Christmas Eve.

"Oh, look at the cute deer," Morgan said. "I wonder how they get their eyelashes to look so long and curly. Do you think they use mascara?"

"I doubt it," Sabrina told her. "It would be pretty hard to apply mascara with a hoof."

"Why am I dreaming about deer?" Roxie murmured. "Especially deer locked up in a pen?"

"Um, when you wake up you'll have to look in one of those what-do-your-dreams-mean books and find out," Sabrina urged.

"Must have been those couple of hours I put in with Santa at the mall," Roxie said. "I've never dreamed anything like this before."

"This is no dream and those are not deer," Miles said excitedly. "We've been kidnapped by aliens and taken to their planet." He pointed to Rudolph. "How else would you explain that reindeer with the bright red nose?"

"Aachoo!" Morgan sneezed. "It's cold in my dream. I'm going to have to add a warmer comforter to my Christmas list."

"Are presents the only thing you can dream about?" Roxie asked her.

"Well, getting presents is what Christmas is all about, isn't it?" Morgan asked her.

"What about *giving*?" Sabrina said. "I thought this is the time of the year when it's better to give than to receive."

"That's right," Morgan agreed. "And I want everyone to be happy. So if people get joy from giving, I'll be glad to receive."

Sabrina chuckled to herself. Morgan was about to be on the other side of that giving and receiving equation. Maybe she'd realize how wonderful it felt to do things for other people once in a while.

"Come on, you guys," Sabrina urged. "Let's take this dream sequence inside." She opened the door to the Workshop and stepped aside to let her friends enter.

Santa's Workshop was in high gear as Sabrina and her roommates entered the room. The elves were hard at work making toys. They moved so quickly they looked like little green, red, and white blurs racing around. Some were sawing wood to make boats, cars, baseball bats, and checkers and chess sets. Others were carefully styling doll hair and making sure that each doll dress was perfectly snapped and buttoned. Still other elves were busy making sure that computer games worked without glitches.

"Whoo-hoo!" one elf exclaimed. "I made it to the seventh level."

Sabrina laughed. The computer game section was definitely a newer addition to Santa's Workshop.

"Whoa! Would you look at this?!" Miles exclaimed.

"Has anyone noticed that all these elves are dressed exactly alike?" Morgan asked. "I wonder if they planned it that way."

"They're working awfully hard—I hope they've got a union to make sure they're paid overtime," Roxie added.

"Oh, I think they're treated just fine," Sabrina assured her. "Their boss is a very benevolent guy."

"The term is 'supervisor,' Sabrina," Roxie corrected her. "No one is the boss of anyone else."

At that moment, the elves' supervisor walked over to the group. Santa looked curiously at Sabrina but said nothing. Rufus, the elf who seemed permanently glued to Santa's side, was not as quiet.

"Not you again," Rufus moaned. "What are you going to do now—ask to borrow the reindeer for a little late night sky cruise?"

"Oh no," Sabrina assured him. "I'm not here to ask for anything. We've come to help."

"I think you've done quite enough already," Rufus replied.

"Now Rufus, Sabrina is our guest," Santa reminded the elf.

"An uninvited guest," Rufus added.

"Still," Santa said. "Let's hear her out."

"You said you needed a few more elves to help you finish your toy quota before Christmas Eve," Sabrina began.

"Which is tomorrow night," Rufus reminded her.

"I know. So there's no time to waste. That's why I've brought you some new elves."

Rufus stared at Morgan, Roxie, and Miles. "They don't look like elves to me." He pointed to the green face cream on Morgan's face. "What is this one—some sort of mutant leprechaun? Wrong holiday, Sabrina."

Sabrina quickly pointed at Morgan, and her face cream disappeared. She smiled at Rufus. "My friends and I are ready to help make toys." She turned to Santa. "Will four more people be enough to get all the toys made in time?"

"I'm not sure," Santa admitted honestly. "But we sure can use any help we can get." He turned toward Miles, Roxie, and Morgan.

"Are you ready to make toys?" he asked them.

"Wow! This is some dream," Miles said.

Santa looked at him curiously. "Dream?"

"He means a dream come true," Sabrina butted in. "Who wouldn't think meeting Santa is a dream come true? You're a huge celebrity."

"True," Santa agreed.

"I've never actually helped anyone before," Morgan admitted. "But I guess since this is just a dream . . ."

"Do you use all biodegradable materials in this shop?" Roxie interrupted. "I don't want to be involved in making anything that will destroy the planet."

Santa thought for a moment. "I can't promise that we don't use any plastic," he admitted. "It's a safer material for some of the babies. But I can make certain that you're stationed at an all-natural workbench."

"That'll do," Roxie said. "Just point me in the right direction."

"Rufus, take her over to where Carlos and Jackson are carving boats," Santa said. "What would you like to do?" he asked Miles.

"Those computer games look like fun," he replied.

"Good," Santa said. "You can help pack up the

disks. Make sure the directions go into all the packages. The booklets are pretty thick—we've had the instructions translated into seven languages."

"What about Morgan?" Sabrina asked.

"Doll clothes!" Morgan begged. "Please. I love dressing dolls!"

Santa smiled. "Great! Just go over to Mrs. Claus, and she'll get you started." The jolly guy pointed to his equally jolly wife, who was across the room fitting tiny, pink high heels onto an 11½-inch fashion doll.

"No! Wait!" Morgan called over to Mrs. Claus. "You don't want pink shoes with a yellow dress. In fact, you might not want her to wear a yellow dress at all. It doesn't go with her skin tone or her hair color."

Mrs. Claus shot her husband a desperate look, but Santa pretended not to notice.

"Okay, now how about me? What can I do?" Sabrina asked Santa.

Santa sighed. "I think you should just try and stay out of trouble."

Sabrina frowned. She deserved that. But she really did want to help. "Come on, Santa, there must be something I can do."

Santa thought for a moment. Then he called over

to one of his elves. "Hey, Rick. Get Sabrina an extra jacket."

"Why am I going to need that?" she asked him.

"It's pretty cold where you'll be working," Santa told her.

A few minutes later, Sabrina found herself in the reindeer pen, with a thick red coat buttoned up to her neck and a pail and shovel in hand.

"Make sure you get out all of the reindeer manure," Rick, the elf who had brought her the coat, told her. "Santa likes to keep his property clean."

It was hours before anyone came out to check on Sabrina. But she'd been too busy to look at the time, anyway. Nine reindeer can make a big mess! Finally Roxie appeared at the gate to the reindeer pen.

"I brought you some hot cider," she said, handing Sabrina a mug.

Sabrina gratefully took the cup from Roxie's hands. "Thank you. I could really use something warm," she said through shivering lips. But as Sabrina raised the mug to her lips, a block of apple-flavored ice bonked her in the face.

"It was hot when I poured it," Roxie vowed.

"That's okay," Sabrina assured her. "I understand."

Roxie wrinkled up her nose. "It stinks out here. How can you stand it?"

"I think my nose is frozen," Sabrina told her. "Just like the rest of me."

"Good thing this is all a dream, huh?" Roxie said. "Otherwise you'd have one heck of a cold after being out here in the North Pole night air."

"Yeah, good thing," Sabrina muttered. "Aaaachoo!"

"Gesundheit. Too bad you're not inside with us," she continued. "It's a lot of fun. You know, for the first time I see what you mean about the spirit of Christmas. It's kind of a kick to know that some kid will be opening up a gift I made on Christmas morning."

"What are you making?" Sabrina asked her.

"Well, I started out carving boats," Roxie said.

"Sounds like something you'd like."

Roxie nodded. "But now I'm wrapping toy trucks and boats. I'm getting pretty fast, too. I had a wrapping contest with some of the elves, and I came in fourth."

"That's great!" Sabrina cheered. "How many of you were in the contest?"

"Uh, four," Roxie coughed into her hand, trying to muffle her response.

"How many?" Sabrina asked again. "I couldn't hear you."

"Four. Okay?" Roxie sounded annoyed. "But I'm so much faster than I was when I started. They only finished a few seconds before me."

"That's terrific."

"And you should see Morgan," Roxie continued. "She's really getting into the Christmas spirit thing. She's been designing clothes for all the dolls. She puts a little tag in the dresses that says, 'Made with Love from Morgan.'"

"Wow!" Sabrina exclaimed. "That I'd like to see."

"It's like she's been transformed. And Miles is really into it, too. He just taught the elves a song about a Hanukkah dreidel. Well, I've gotta get going," Roxie said. "Mrs. Claus has promised us all a cookie break, and then it's back to wrapping more gifts. Rufus promised that during his next break he'd teach me some new verses to that song about Rudolph here. Apparently they're not rated for general audiences."

As Roxie went back inside for more cookies and caroling, Sabrina picked up a reindeer-sized pooper scooper. "Back to work," she sighed.

Chapter 11

It was almost dawn on Christmas Eve when Santa finally walked out to the reindeer pen. Well, it would have been dawn, but in December, the North Pole is pretty much dark all year long. Since Sabrina's watch had frozen long before, she had no idea how long she'd been out there.

"I have good news for you," Santa greeted her with a hearty smile. "The gifts are finished. We have just enough for all the good boys and girls. Your friends were marvelous. I'm going to make sure there's a little something extra in their stockings this year."

Sabrina tried to manage a smile, but her lips were frozen. "I suppose I'm getting a lump of coal," she muttered.

Santa wrapped one of his big arms around her

shoulders, and Sabrina nuzzled close. Santa was warm in a magical way. Just being near him took away the frostbite and chills that she'd felt all night. "I think you're a good witch, Sabrina," he assured her. "You make mistakes. We all do. But you took responsibility for yours. That takes your name off the naughty list and puts you at the top of my nice list."

"Thanks, Santa. I needed that."

Santa nodded. "We all need a pat on the back once in a while. Your friends also needed to find a little holiday spirit. You gave them that tonight. If you never give them another gift, that'll be enough."

Gift! Sabrina's eyes opened wide. It was Christmas Eve. In a few hours she would have to give Miles his Secret Santa gift. She had so much to do—go to the mall, pick up her check, get to the science store for the telescope lens . . .

Quickly Sabrina turned and ran into Santa's Workshop. Santa followed close behind.

The Workshop was strangely quiet, compared to the bedlam the night before. The gifts were all wrapped, and two elves were busy putting them into Santa's big red sack. The other elves were quietly resting by the fire, sipping hot chocolate and munching on Mrs. Claus's sugar cookies.

Sabrina looked around for her friends. She found Miles sitting beside an elf. He was studying the elf's pointy little ears. "You know, if you were a little taller, and didn't have any emotions, you could pass for Mr. Spock," he told him.

"Mr. who?" the elf asked.

"Mr. Spock, from the old TV show *Star Trek*. He had pointy ears, too."

The elf shrugged. "We don't watch TV up here. There's no cable and we get lousy reception."

As Miles chatted with his elf buddy, Morgan sat with Mrs. Claus. She was brushing the older woman's long white locks. "Have you ever considered coloring your hair? Maybe a nice honey blonde with ash highlights? It would take years off of you."

Roxie was busy as well. She was meeting with a group of elves in the far corner of the room. "I don't think Santa would be angry if you organized a union," she told them. "Actually he's a very fair man. I'll bet he's a big proponent of fair wages for hard work. And you really should have medical insurance, just in case. . . ."

Sabrina walked over to her roommate and tapped her on the shoulder. "Okay, Norma Rae," she teased, referring to the old movie about a union organizer.

"I think we should be getting back home."

"Back?" Roxie replied. "But I was just about to ask Santa if I could ride with him tonight and help him deliver gifts."

"You?" Sabrina asked, surprised. "I never thought of you as the kind of girl who'd want to ride shotgun in a sleigh."

Roxie shrugged. "I guess I'm just filled with the Christmas spirit."

"Well, we have to take that spirit home," Sabrina told her. "Come on, Miles and Morgan," she added. "It's almost time to wake up from this dream."

Slowly Morgan and Miles walked over toward Sabrina and Roxie. "You know, this has been the strangest dream," Morgan told her. "I wasn't stranded on a desert island with Ashton Kutcher for even an instant."

"Is that what most of your dreams are like?" Roxie asked.

Morgan nodded. "Aren't everyone's?"

Sabrina raised her finger. "Speaking of dreams," she said as she got ready to zap everyone home.

"This night has been a dream come true.
Now Santa can do what he needs to do.

*But it's time for these human elves to go away,
And let Santa get ready to drive his sleigh."*

In a flash Sabrina and her friends were back in their off-campus house. She made sure each of her friends was right back where she'd found them—Roxie curled up in her bed, Morgan sleeping face up with a new coat of green face cream, and Miles cuddling his tribble. Then she got ready to get into bed and catch a few winks herself.

But before Sabrina could snuggle down under the covers, her alarm clock went off. It was time for work.

"Good morning!" Roxie sat up in bed and greeted Sabrina.

Sabrina stared at her roommate, shocked. Roxie was not a morning person. But today, she was bright eyed and ready to face the world.

"What are you doing up so early?" Sabrina asked her.

"It's Christmas Eve. I'm so excited. I've got a lot to do before tonight," Roxie told her. Then she stopped for a second. "Did I just say that?"

Sabrina laughed. "Looks like you've got a little bit of Christmas spirit. I wonder where that came from."

"I had the weirdest dream last night," Roxie began. "I was at Santa's Workshop. You were there."

"I was?" Sabrina asked innocently.

Roxie nodded. "Morgan and Miles, too. We were helping the elves make gifts."

"Wow, that *is* a weird dream," Sabrina replied. She sneezed. Then sneezed again.

"Sounds like you're getting a cold," Roxie said. "Probably from being outside in the cold air for so long."

Sabrina looked at her curiously, but she was careful not to say anything.

"I guess that was part of my dream, too," Roxie continued. "I'm telling you, it was so real. I could even smell the candy canes and the cookies baking in Mrs. Claus's oven. . . ." Roxie began. Then she sniffed at the air. "Speaking of smells, what's that?"

"What?"

"I don't know," Roxie told her. "It smells like a petting zoo."

Sabrina gulped. "Um, I don't smell anything," she said as she quickly picked dirty clothes off the floor and threw them in the hamper. "I've got to take a shower before work."

By the time Sabrina was showered and dressed in her elf costume, her roommates were all awake. They were sitting together at the kitchen table.

"Better make that coffee double strong," Morgan said. "I feel like I've barely been asleep."

"I know what you mean," Miles agreed. He held up his hands. "And it's the strangest thing. I woke up this morning with all these paper cuts."

"They're probably from stuffing all those instruction packets into the computer game boxes," Roxie murmured as she poured water into the coffeemaker.

Miles looked at her with surprise. "How'd you know about that?" he asked.

Roxie shook her head. "I'm sorry, it was just something that happened in this weird dream I had."

"You had a weird dream, too?" Miles asked her. "You wouldn't believe what I was dreaming last night. I was up at the North Pole and—"

"Um, I've got to get going," Sabrina interrupted. "My last day at work. Then I pick up my check and go get my Secret Santa gift." She smiled broadly, taking care not to look directly at Miles.

"I already got the gift for the person whose name I chose," Morgan said. "I think a certain someone is going to be very happy tonight."

"Funny," Miles added. "I was just thinking the same thing."

Roxie poured herself a cup of coffee and headed back into the room she shared with Sabrina. "I've got to get going on my gift," she said. Then she burst into song. "He knows when you've been sleeping, he knows when you're awake, he knows if you've been bad or good, so you'd better be good for goodness sake. . . ." She stopped mid-song. "Did I just sing that?" she wondered aloud.

Sabrina's last day at the Santa's Workshop in the mall was bittersweet. After visiting the real North Pole, this imitation Santa's Workshop didn't seem very magical. The cardboard and cotton snow were chipping away and looked old and worn. Already some of the Christmas lights had burned out in the tree display, and the mechanical Rudolph's red nose had long since stopped glowing. But hey, at least he didn't leave a mess for the elves to clean up!

Barney didn't hold a candle to the real Santa either. Weeks of having children drool and spit up on him had left him tired and a little cantankerous.

Still, not everything at the Santa's Workshop photo shop was fake. Sabrina knew she'd miss the genuine joy on the kids' faces when they got their first close-up look into Santa's eyes.

Sabrina was also looking forward to her paycheck. She knew that the smiles on the kids' faces would soon be replaced with the smile on Miles's face when he opened his Secret Santa gift and found his Mirror Reflective Telescope Lens. That would make the whole experience worth it.

"Well, that about wraps it up," Stan said as the clock on the wall read 5:30. "The mall's closing early tonight for Christmas Eve."

Sabrina gasped. "But the mall can't close early!" she shouted. "I still have one gift to buy."

Stan handed her a check for the work she'd done. "Too late now," he said. "The stores are all closed."

Sabrina's eyes welled up with tears. "But they can't be closed," she murmured as she made her way out of the building and into the parking lot. Sabrina felt awful. This whole Secret Santa thing had been her idea, and now she was the only one who wouldn't have a gift to give. She sat down on a bench in a secluded part of the mall and began to cry.

"Ho-ho-ho, Merry Christmas!" A deep booming voice came up behind her.

"I'm not in the mood, Barney," Sabrina mumbled, thinking it was the mall Santa playing a trick on her.

"Beg your pardon? I've been called St. Nick, Santa Claus, even Bob, but never Barney."

Sabrina whipped around and looked up into the kindest blue eyes she'd ever seen. "Oh, Santa, it's you! I'm sorry. I thought . . ."

"I know, you thought I was one of my many look-alikes. It's okay."

Sabrina shook her head. "No, it's not. Nothing's okay. I worked so hard, and now I can't even get Miles his Secret Santa gift."

"I heard," Santa said. "The mall closed early. No one wants to work on Christmas Eve—except me, of course." He sat down beside Sabrina on the bench. "Maybe I can help."

"I don't think so," Sabrina told him.

"Well, I just happen to have a Mirror Reflective Telescope Lens in my sack," Santa hinted.

Sabrina sat up tall. "You do?"

Santa nodded. "And I'd be willing to give it to you if . . ."

"If what?"

"Well, remember I told you that by helping me out you'd earned a nice gift on Christmas?"

Sabrina smiled. "Who could forget that?"

"Well, here's the deal," Santa continued. "I also have a gorgeous lavender sweater in my sack with your name on it."

"The one I saw in the window of Olshan's Department Store?" Sabrina asked eagerly. "I've been dying to own that one."

"I know," Santa told her. "And you can have it tonight. Unless you'd rather trade it for the telescope lens. Remember, I told you: You can't take without replacing."

Sabrina didn't even have to think. She'd find another way to get the sweater. Or she'd live without it. But seeing Miles's face when he opened that package would be a great Christmas gift. "I'd rather have the lens," she told Santa.

That brought a huge grin to St. Nick's broad, cheery face. "I knew you'd say that," he said. "You have the true Christmas spirit. Why I'll bet you even got something wonderful for that cat of yours!"

"Salem!" Sabrina exclaimed. "Oh no!" With all her thoughts of Secret Santa, she'd forgotten to get gifts for Salem and her aunts. "I still need gifts for Aunt Hilda and Aunt Zelda, too."

"I think the hardware store on Elm Street is still

open," Santa said as he handed Sabrina the telescope lens. "They never close. Maybe you can find something for them there."

"Thanks, Santa," Sabrina said sincerely. "For everything."

"You're welcome," he replied. "But I've got to get going now. I've got a long transcontinental flight ahead of me."

Chapter 12

"**M**erry Christmas, everyone!" Sabrina shouted as she entered Zelda and Hilda's house. "I come bearing gifts!"

"If it isn't our favorite niece!" Zelda said as she walked out into the living room to greet her.

Sabrina laughed. "Your only niece." She handed each of her aunts a gift. "I hope you like these."

"Christmas presents! Oh goodie!" Hilda squealed.

"Sabrina, you shouldn't have," Zelda said as she unwrapped her gift. "A toilet plunger?" she asked, surprised. "You *really* shouldn't have!"

"It's not just a plunger," Sabrina assured her aunt.

Zelda looked at the black rubber half-sphere attached to the end of a wooden stick. It certainly looked like a plunger. "It's not?"

"No. It's a symbol of the chores I'm going to do for you around here. My gift to you is free cleaning for a week. And that includes the bathrooms!"

Zelda smiled. "I would love that. Not having to clean would definitely give me more time for my experiments." She gave Sabrina a hug.

"Now let's see what I got," Hilda said as she shook the small box in her hands. "We all know good things come in small packages. I got a . . . combination lock?"

"It's not just a lock," Sabrina said. "It's the lock I'm going to use on the door to the coffeehouse."

"But I don't even know the combination," Hilda said.

"I know," Sabrina told her. "But I do. And I'm going to open the coffeehouse for two weeks. That way you can sleep late."

"Ooh, the gift of sleep. I like that!" Hilda exclaimed as she gave Sabrina a peck on the cheek.

"We have something for you, as well," Zelda said. She reached down under the tree and pulled out a rectangular box wrapped in red-and-green Christmas paper.

Sabrina tore open the box with gusto. "I love Christmas!" Her smile grew even bigger when she saw what was inside. "The lavender sweater from Olshan's Department Store! It's just what I wanted."

Zelda smiled. "A little bird told us you might like it."

"Actually, a big chubby bird with a long white beard who owns only one suit," Hilda added.

"But Santa said . . ."

Zelda put her arm around Sabrina. "I know, Santa said that you had to exchange the sweater for Miles's gift. But he never said that Hilda and I couldn't go to the store and buy it for you. This sweater comes from a mortal store, not Santa's private gift stock."

"But all the stores were closed," Sabrina said.

Zelda smiled. "Not the stores in California. They're three hours behind us, remember. We zapped there just a few minutes ago, got the sweater, and zapped back."

"Santa thought you deserved to get something you wanted this Christmas, since you've been so busy thinking about others," Hilda added.

Just then Salem came hobbling down the stairs. He moved slowly, with one leg draped over a little kitty crutch to help him walk with all of his injuries. "Did you forget me?" he asked.

"Never!" Sabrina assured him. "I just couldn't carry yours. It's out on the porch." She walked over and opened the door. Sitting on the porch was the largest ball of twine Salem had ever seen.

"It was the biggest supply of string they had in the hardware store," Sabrina assured him.

Salem smiled . . . a little. "Well, I'd leap into your arms and thank you," he assured Sabrina. "But I'm at least eight weeks and several physical therapy sessions away from leaping."

Sabrina nodded understandingly. "Speaking of which, have you heard from the judges of the Favorite Familiars Calendar Contest?"

Salem moaned slightly. "That was the biggest injury of all," he told her. "I didn't win."

"Oh no!" Sabrina exclaimed genuinely. "They chose Alexander the Not So Great as Mr. April?"

Salem shook his little head. At least Sabrina thought he'd shaken his head—it was hard to tell with his little kitty whiplash collar.

"The judges said that Alexander and I were too beat up to look good in any photographs. And they said that these days women had changed their views on what was considered sexy. They said women preferred a different kind of familiar."

"What kind of familiar is that?" Sabrina asked.

"Would you believe the sensitive bookish type of guy?" Salem asked. "I mean do you know any woman who would prefer that to me?"

"Well, I would," Zelda broke in.

"Okay, well, that's one. But I'm sure you're in the minority," Salem told her.

"Actually, Salem," Sabrina said, "I kind of like a guy who cries at sad movies and reads good books. It gives us something in common."

"And I think—" Hilda began.

"Okay! Enough already!" Salem shouted. "I get the point."

"So who did they pick?" Sabrina asked him.

"Lenny!" Salem exclaimed. "Lenny the Lizard!"

At that moment Lenny came slithering down the stairs, holding a long contract in his claws. "Did someone call me?" he asked.

"No, you traitor!" Salem replied.

"Oh, come on, Salem," Lenny said. "Be a good sport. Besides, you can tell everyone that you're a close friend of Mr. April—that's bound to give you some pull with the women!" The lizard turned to Sabrina. "You wouldn't happen to know a good modeling agent, would you?" he asked. "I think I could have a whole new career after this."

Salem hissed in Lenny's direction and hobbled back up the stairs. He was in such a bad mood, Sabrina didn't have the heart to ask if he'd gotten her anything for Christmas. Besides, she had a feeling she knew the answer to that one.

Sabrina arrived back at her college house just a few minutes before midnight. Her eyes opened wide as she walked into the living room. There were colored lights hung all around the windowsills and door frames. Simple white candles sat on the kitchen counters. "Silent Night" was blaring from the stereo. It was obvious that her roommates' late night journey to the North Pole had done a lot to instill the Christmas spirit into them.

"Well, look who's here," Roxie said. "We were beginning to think you'd forgotten about us."

"Never!" Sabrina assured her. She pointed to her purse. "I've got my Secret Santa gift right here."

Morgan walked up to Sabrina holding a tray of cookies. Sabrina looked at her with surprise. The usually stylish Morgan had her hair up in a decidedly matronly tight bun, and she was wearing a frilly red and green apron that said SANTA'S SPECIAL

HELPER. She looked strangely like a younger version of Mrs. Claus.

"Christmas cookie?" she offered Sabrina.

Sabrina hesitated for a moment. The sugar cookies, shaped like Christmas trees, stars, and little Santa Clauses, did look delicious. But . . .

"You didn't actually bake these, did you Morgan?"

Morgan shook her head. "I bought them at the supermarket. Can you imagine me baking?" she asked Sabrina.

"I can't imagine you in a supermarket," Miles interjected.

Sabrina giggled as she took a Christmas tree shaped cookie from the tray.

"Okay, enough of this," Roxie interrupted. "Let's exchange gifts. I can't wait to see what my Secret Santa's going to say when she sees what I've got for her."

"She, huh? Well, I guess that lets me out," Miles said. "Roxie obviously picked one of your two names from the hat."

Sabrina reached into her pocketbook and pulled out Miles's gift. "That's okay, Miles," she assured him. "I chose your name. And I think you're going to love what I got you."

Miles took the package from Sabrina and tore open the wrapping. His eyes grew wide when he discovered what was inside. "Oh, my gosh!" he exclaimed. "I've wanted this forever. I love you, Sabrina!" Then, realizing what he'd said, Miles quickly added, "In a purely platonic way, of course."

"Of course," Sabrina assured him.

"My turn! My turn!" Morgan shouted. She ran into her room and came out with a box with a big red bow on it. "Roxie, this is for you," she said.

"Wow, Morgan, I can't believe you picked my name from the hat," Roxie said as she opened the box.

"Neither could I, when it happened. But then I saw this and . . ."

Roxie frowned slightly as she pulled the gift from the box. It was a dress—the exact same dress she and Sabrina had seen Morgan looking at in the boutique in the mall. The dress was pale pink and very feminine. It was distinctly Morgan's style—and definitely not Roxie's.

Roxie wasn't great at hiding disappointment. She stared at the dress in frustration. Then she peeked at the tag that was affixed to the side of the dress. "This isn't even my size," she moaned.

"It's not?" Morgan asked in mock surprise. She took the dress from Roxie and held it up to her own body. "What do you know? It's exactly *my* size."

Roxie rolled her eyes. "Gee, what a surprise."

Morgan thought for a moment. Finally she said, "You know what, Roxie? I have a great idea!"

"Let me guess," Roxie said. "You'll keep the dress."

"Exactly," Morgan agreed. "Especially since it's not returnable. No sale items are."

"How convenient for you," Roxie replied.

"But I'm not going to leave you without a gift," Morgan assured her.

"You're not?" Roxie sounded suspicious.

"No," Morgan assured her. "As soon as the stores open on December 26, you and I will go to the fabric store. You can pick out any cloth you want. Then I will make a special outfit, just for you. An original Morgan."

Roxie was stunned. Morgan was a wonderful designer. Her home-sewn outfits were the envy of everyone on campus. But Morgan had never offered to make an outfit for any of her roommates before. "Wow!" Roxie exclaimed. "That's a great present, Morgan!"

But Morgan was already focused on her own new dress. "It is, isn't it?" she murmured, looking at the pastel pink fabric.

"I've got a gift for you, Morgan," Miles said.

That brought Morgan back to the task at hand. "You do?" she asked eagerly, holding her hands out.

"It's a day at a spa!" Miles exclaimed as he handed her a white envelope.

"Oh Miles, just what I w—" Morgan began. She stopped as she pulled a green gift certificate from the envelope. "What's this?" she demanded. "This isn't a gift certificate from Zen Zone."

Miles shook his head. "No, this is a gift certificate from Amazing Aliens."

"That science fiction shop?" Morgan sounded horrified.

Miles nodded. "They have a great spa in the back. I've signed you up for a full regimen."

"Regimen of what?"

"You'll start with a Martian mud bath that's given to you in a rocket ship shaped room," Miles told her. "I knew you'd like that, since you wear that green stuff on your face every night."

"How did you know that?" Morgan asked. "No one sees me like that."

"I'm not sure, I just know it," Miles began. "Unless I dreamed it. . . ."

"That must be it," Sabrina butted in. "You dreamed it. Go on, Miles, what else does Morgan get?"

"A Venutian love goddess aromatherapy facial, and a purple Pluto pedicure," he announced.

"They put purple polish on my toes?" Morgan asked.

"I think it's more like lavender," Miles said. "I've never actually done that one."

Roxie started to laugh as she pictured Miles rolling around in a mud bath and getting a facial. "You mean you've been to this spa before?"

"Hey," Miles replied, "can't a guy care about how he looks?"

Roxie was about to make a crack about Miles's usual semi-sloppy appearance, but Sabrina stopped her.

"Of course he can, Miles," Sabrina interrupted. "I like guys who are in touch with their more sensitive side. I was just telling Salem . . ."

"You were talking to your cat?" Roxie asked her.

Oops! Once again Sabrina had started to say too much. "Uh, sure," Sabrina said. "Doesn't everyone?"

"I guess it would be nice to tell your thoughts to someone who can't answer back," Roxie admitted.

"I wish," Sabrina muttered.

Morgan fingered the spa gift certificate for a moment. "Mud bath, facial, pedicure . . . hmmm . . . not bad, Miles."

Miles's face brightened. "Really?" he asked excitedly. "Not bad? Wow! I can't believe you like my gift, Morgan. I was so worried."

"Whoa, Miles, slow down," Morgan warned. "Let's not jump to any conclusions. I said it wasn't bad. I didn't say I liked it. At least not yet. I reserve judgment for after the beauty treatment."

"Hey, I ordered a gift certificate for myself while I was calling for yours," Miles told her. "Maybe we could go together."

Morgan shot Miles a look. "I don't think so."

Sabrina grinned slightly when she heard Miles say he'd called for the gift certificate. Purple nail polish, mud bath, rocket ship room, aromatherapy. Obviously that was what he'd been doing that afternoon when Sabrina had caught him on the phone. He'd been busy ordering Morgan's gift.

One mystery solved.

But that still didn't explain why Roxie had acted

so strange that same afternoon, skulking around the mall, pretending to forget where Sabrina worked, and throwing that mysterious piece of black plastic into her bag. Unless . . .

Of course! Sabrina smiled broadly. Roxie still hadn't given out her Secret Santa gift. Since everyone else had gotten their gifts, it was clear that Roxie was Sabrina's Secret Santa. Her weird behavior at the mall must have had something to do with that. Roxie must have been buying Sabrina a gift that afternoon. That was what the small black object must have been.

Roxie held out a gift. Sabrina was ready for a small, black package. But Roxie's gift was too big to fit into her small purse. Instead it was shaped like a large book and wrapped in newspaper.

"What's that? A dead fish?" Morgan asked.

"Excuse me?" Roxie asked her, menacingly.

"Well, that's the only thing I know of that you'd wrap in old newspapers," Morgan explained.

"It's recycyled wrapping paper. I'm sure Sabrina appreciates the sentiment."

Sabrina grinned. "It's a gift for me and the planet."

"Exactly," Roxie said. "Anyhow, it's nothing expensive, because, as you know, I didn't have a whole lot of success on the job front during this holiday season."

"That's okay," Sabrina assured her. "It's the thought that counts. I'm sure I'll love it."

Sabrina unwrapped the gift. Inside the newspaper was a photo album. Roxie had used red and green glitter to write the words "Sabrina at the North Pole" on the front.

"It's photos I've taken," Roxie explained.

Sabrina was afraid to open the book. Had Roxie actually taken photos of her during their late night visit to Santa's home? That meant that there was proof that she and her roommates had actually been there—that it hadn't been a dream.

"I, uh, think I'll open this later. You know, in private," Sabrina said quickly.

"No way!" Morgan cried out, grabbing the book from Sabrina's hands. "This I gotta see!" She opened the book and peeked inside "I knew it!" she declared. "I just knew it!"

"Knew what?" Sabrina asked, trying to keep her voice as calm as possible.

"Just that you weren't all smiles and joy this holiday season." Morgan laughed. She handed the book to Sabrina. "Take a look!"

Sabrina looked down at the first page of the photo album. There was a snapshot of her holding a baby up to Barney, the mall Santa. It was obvious the baby had a dirty diaper, since both Sabrina and Barney seemed to be rejecting the tiny tot, and both had their noses wrinkled up in an effort not to breathe. The baby, however, seemed positively ecstatic. Sabrina gave a sigh of relief. Roxie had meant the Santa's Workshop at the mall.

"And look at this one," Miles said, pointing to a picture at the bottom of the page in which Sabrina was busy pulling a cherry lollipop from her hair. "That's an interesting hairdo, Sabrina."

"More like a hair-don't!" Morgan teased.

Sabrina laughed. She turned the page. There was a picture of a child yanking Barney's beard. There was also a picture of a happy child hugging Sabrina.

"This is the best gift I've ever gotten," she told Roxie. "I love it. But when did you manage to put this whole thing together?"

"I got the idea after Stan fired me. I mean, those parents didn't have to pay him for photos. They could have taken them all themselves. Not only would it have been cheaper, it would've been more personal."

"That's true," Sabrina agreed.

"So I just bought one of those disposable cameras at the drugstore and followed you around for a couple of days," Roxie continued. "It was actually kind of fun. You got yourself into some real messes. It was kind of like watching a real-life sitcom."

"So that was what you were doing when I bumped into you at the mall," Sabrina mused.

Roxie nodded. "That one was close. You almost caught me. I had the camera out and everything. I slipped it into my bag just in time. I didn't know what to say. I acted so stupid, I was sure you'd figured out that I was your Secret Santa."

"I'm glad I didn't figure it out," Sabrina admitted. "This is a great surprise! I'll treasure it always."

"Well, if we're all finished exchanging gifts, I'm going to try out my new telescope lens. It's a really clear night. I'm going to see all kinds of things up there," Miles exclaimed, his eyes glowing with sheer joy. He took his gift and bounded into his room. A few seconds later, he returned with his telescope. "I'm going out to the backyard," he told the others, "if anyone else wants to take a look."

But the girls seemed more interested in Roxie's photos than the constellations. As Miles set up his telescope, Sabrina, Roxie, and Morgan continued to look at the pictures in Sabrina's photo album.

"Oh, there's a nice one," Morgan giggled as she pointed to a shot of a little boy kicking Sabrina in the knees. Sabrina's face was about ·as red as her costume, and her eyes seemed to be bulging out of her head.

"I should have gotten combat pay for that one," Sabrina told her. "I'm still black and blue."

"Why was he so upset?" Roxie asked her.

"I think Santa told him that he couldn't trade his little sister for a horse," Sabrina explained. "I'm telling you, kids asked for the strangest things. One little girl asked Santa to bring her a new name!"

"Why?" Roxie asked.

"She said there were three Samanthas in her class and she wanted to be different," Sabrina explained.

"What name did she want?" Morgan asked.

"Cellophane."

"You mean like the plastic wrap?" Morgan asked.

Sabrina nodded. "She thought it sounded pretty."

"She thought wrong," Morgan assured her. "No wonder Santa refused to bring her a new name."

"I can't believe the kids fell for that Barney guy

being Santa," Roxie said. "He doesn't even look anything like the real Santa."

"I know what you mean," Morgan admitted. "His eyes aren't nearly as bright, and his belly isn't at all like a bowl full of jelly. It's stuffed with pillows! And of course the real Santa is much more handsome."

Morgan and Roxie stared at each other for a moment, each realizing what the other had said.

"I mean, that's what I've *heard*," Morgan covered quickly, not wanting her friends to think she actually believed in Santa Claus. After all, it had all been a dream. She was sure of that.

"Of course," Roxie said just as quickly. "That's what I meant, too."

Sabrina stifled a giggle and turned the page. But before she could look at another photo, Miles called from the yard.

"Sabrina, Roxie, Morgan come out here right away!" he shouted. "You guys are never going to believe this."

The girls raced out to the yard. Miles had his telescope pointing straight up into the night sky. "Take a look at what's up there," he said as he stepped aside to give someone else a peek.

"What is it? A comet?" Roxie asked.

"A meteor?" Morgan guessed.

"No," Miles told them. "It's Santa Claus!"

Roxie's face fell. "Very funny, Miles."

"Yeah, what do you take us for?" Morgan asked.

Miles looked helplessly at his roommates. "But I swear I saw him riding in a sleigh."

"I'm going back in," Roxie said, wrapping her arms across her chest. "It's freezing out here."

"Right behind you," Morgan agreed. "Let's take a look at some designs for that new dress I'm going to make for you."

"Cool," Roxie agreed. "I'm looking for something really different."

"Why am I not surprised," Morgan said.

As the girls went into the house, Miles followed, pleading with them to believe him. "But I'm not kidding," he swore. "I saw him, and the sleigh, and all the reindeer."

"Stop it, Miles," Morgan replied.

Once everyone else was inside, Sabrina took the opportunity to look into Miles's telescope. The stars were bright and beautiful, but she saw no sign of St. Nicholas driving by. Was it possible Miles was just teasing?

And then she saw a bright red light against the dark sky. Sabrina grinned. There was no mistaking that light, she'd watched it glow the whole night she'd been at the North Pole. That was Rudolph's nose! Sure enough, behind Rudolph came the other flying reindeer, their legs moving back and forth at top speed, pulling the heavy sleigh across the sky, looking for the next roof to land on.

As Santa flew by, he called out to the faithful: "Merry Christmas to all, and to all a good night!"